DIRTY *Red* DIAMONDS

WELCOME TO SIN CITY.

Vogue

Crown Jewelz Publishing

Dirty Red Diamonds
Part VII of The Diamond Collection
Copyright © 2022 Vogue

ISBN-13: 978-0-9888004-7-2

Cover Design by Vogue

Website: www.simplyvogue.net
Instagram: iam_carmendavenport

Other Works in The Diamond Collection

ACKNOWLEDGEMENTS

With almost six years passing since my last book release, publishing two books on the same day would not be possible without my Lord and Savior, Jesus Christ. Your abundant blessings helped me reach this goal.

Next, I would love to thank my editor, Michelle Chester, of EBM Professional Services, for joining me on this journey. Since *The Ace of Diamonds*, you are often the first to read (and critique, lol) my work. I've learned so much from you over the years. Thank you for being a part of The Diamond Collection.

To the Vann family: Jessica, Carl, Jackson, and Streater. Thank you for allowing me to peek inside your world. Watching your interactions as a family, sharing your knowledge as parents, and as professionals, helped a lot of the scenes and characters come to life in *The Diamond Tiara* and *Dirty Red Diamonds*.

To all my readers, thank you for joining me on this ride and for your support. While everything has its own time, I do apologize for the wait.

ONE

Droplets of morning dew stained Carmen's nude flats as she walked away from her parents' graves. One bushel of white roses was in her hands, while another had been left inside the steel vase of her parents' headstone. A short while later, her hands were empty of that bushel, too. This set of roses were left at the grave of her ex-husband's wife, Monifah Kane. She was one of fifteen who was murdered during her company's anniversary party at The Ave less than two weeks ago.

The shooting was the reason she was now making her way out the cemetery. Her ex-husband's former partner, Sanders, agreed to meet with her to discuss how she could aid the case. An employee of the International Triad Intelligence Agency (ITIA), Sanders worked primarily behind a desk due to a previous case, which left him paralyzed.

"Kane told me he talked to you already," was the first thing out Sanders' mouth once she was inside his apartment. Kane, born Michael Kane, had been her husband for about twenty years before they divorced for good. He recently signed a two-year contract with the Triad, and his first assignment was investigating the shooting at The Ave.

"We went over the security footage," Carmen shared. "We never talked about me becoming an agent."

Her words sent Sanders' wheelchair rolling away from his desk. "No, no, no, no, no. Do you want Kane to kill me?" He rolled himself to his front door.

"You say that like you're scared of him."

"Scared of Michael, no, scared of Kane, yes." Sanders undid the lock. "You don't want this. You can't even go in the field. It takes months of training. You gotta pass tests."

His words went on deaf ears. Carmen was writing a check. "What's your price?"

"I'm sorry about what happened to your husband." He spoke of Jay Santiago, the father of three of her seven kids, who was shot four times at the party. "I know you want to find the man who did this. I get it. What's best is if you let us do our jobs. I don't know if Kane told you, but I'm a part of this operation, too."

"What did you say your price was?"

Sanders locked his door. He rolled towards her and peeked at her checkbook. "There are not enough zeros in this world for me to recommend you for the Triad's Training Academy. This isn't a street game. I know you've done your share of dirt, but this is the big leagues."

"Did your girlfriend leave you?"

A look of embarrassment flew over Sanders' face. The question was unexpected.

"Was it too much for her to handle?" Carmen asked. "She didn't like taking care of a man who couldn't walk?" Sanders got quiet on her, the silence telling her she hit the nerve she wanted. "My husband is in a fuckin' hospital bed. He can't talk to me. He can't look at me. He's fuckin' comatose. Do you know what keeps me going? The chance. The chance that one day, whether tomorrow, or five years from now, he'll wake up and see me again. That he'll wake up and see our kids. That's what I'm living for." She glanced at her checkbook before looking at Sanders. "Jay was shot in both his legs. He may not walk again. If he doesn't, I wouldn't love him any less. I'll carry him on my back. This isn't a street game to me. It's love."

Carmen's eyes fell again on her checkbook. "What was your price?"

The only response she got was the sound of Sanders' wheelchair rolling away from her. He went to his desk only to return a minute or so later. This time, he set a notepad on top of her checkbook. A name and address were scribbled on the top page. "Torres Lownes?" she questioned. "Who is he?"

"Your chance," Sanders replied.

That information was all she needed. She thanked him for it as she ripped the page off the notepad. The name wasn't familiar to her, yet that was the least of her worries. Sanders wouldn't put her with anyone he didn't trust. He didn't tell her what Lownes could do for her, but the name was the most she collected in the last few days.

It didn't benefit her to have the lead agent on the case under her roof. The reminder was given to her when she reached the doorway of Kane's bedroom. He was busy packing, although he hadn't told her he was leaving. He'd been staying with her since the shooting at The Ave as he grieved over the loss of his wife. "That quick, huh?" She made her way inside, closing the door behind her. "Y'all must've gotten a good lead."

"We don't have anything," he said. "I gotta get us something." He stopped packing long enough to grab his cell phone. "I'm sending you an email. You can use it to send me pictures and videos of Bella. Don't use it for anything else."

His daughter, Isabella Kane, was a little over three weeks old. Monifah gave birth to her about a week before she was killed. A premature baby, she was currently in the NICU at Brookstone General Hospital. Due to the loss of her mother, at the request of Kane, Carmen now considered the baby her own. In addition to Bella, Carmen and Kane also shared a 19-year-old daughter, Kristian, who was born during their marriage as well as two siblings they adopted, Akaila, who was also 19, and Malachi, a 16-year-old junior at Brookstone High. Her other three children, King, Rakim, and Nyla, were fathered by Jay. King was 21, the oldest of the brood, while Rakim was a few months away from being five and Nyla was four.

"Can you at least tell me where you're going?" she asked him.

"I'm flying to Miami." He threw his phone on the bed, the email now sent. "That's all I can share." He zipped up his duffle bag and set it on the floor.

With the space now free, Carmen moved into it. She was now in front of him. "Have you talked to the kids?" She was speaking of all seven when she posed the question.

"I took them out to breakfast," he shared. "I told 'em then."

"At what time were you gonna tell me?"

The moment he stepped towards the closet, she raised her leg to stop him. Her other leg wrapped around his to hold him in place. "You were just gonna leave, weren't you?"

"Wouldn't it have been for the best?"

Carmen brought her legs down. She knew what he was hinting at. About a week before the party at The Ave, they had a weak moment. They both were going through a tough time with their spouses and was looking for a way to escape. Her garage became the setting of their escapade. Since that night, aside from a small kiss, they hadn't touched each other.

"Is the best goodbye one that's never said?" Her question was intended to give him something to ponder. The phrase, tomorrow isn't promised, didn't need to be uttered. She learned it the hard way when she was 21 and lost her friend, Rakim, during a convenience store shootout. The lesson kept being taught as more losses came. After burying both her parents, Akaila and Malachi's mother, Tricia, and watching her husband fight for his life, she learned all she had was now. Kane knew it, too, which was why, once again, they were peeling off each other's clothes. It was wrong on all accounts, but he owned a place in her heart like her husband. If something were to happen to him, she needed the last goodbye to be one of euphoric ecstasy.

He knew how to send her there, too. He wasn't even inside of her, but he multi-tasked like no other. One set of fingers massaged her pearl, the other circled her left nipple, while his tongue danced with hers. Instead of leading him inside her wetness, her hand sent full strokes up and down his shaft. When her fingertips hit a vein, the feel of it sent her on her knees. The tip of his penis disappeared in her mouth, yet he pulled away before she could taste him.

"What's wrong?" she asked, confused.

"I can't work with this on my head."

He grabbed his boxers and jeans, pulling both up at the same time. "I'll spend this whole operation depressed about what I'm coming home to." He picked up his shirt from the floor.

"We know what it is."

"We know what it isn't," he shot back. "We're telling each other it's sex, but it ain't."

Carmen stared in between them. He was fixing his clothes as if to tell her the tryst was over. Instead of encouraging him to continue, she fixed hers as well. The biggest mistake they made was not having a conversation before they touched. With her dividing her time between sitting at the hospital and home, they barely ran into each other. The growing distance opened Kane's conscience in ways hers hadn't. She knew they were playing a dangerous game. What she didn't know is that her teammate dropped out after the first round. Forced to give up, she left the room in an unwanted manner.

The same could be said for Kane. His plan was to leave the house without seeing her. A note was supposed to be left on the bed for her to find. Somehow, she made it home before his plan was executed. The only reason he stopped her from pleasuring him was to protect himself. A void was in his heart, which she couldn't fill. A few minutes of pleasure couldn't seal the hole Monifah's death created. Not when his body was connecting with a woman who was bound to someone else.

Kane dropped his duffle bag on the ground. He was now outside the estate, surrounded by three of her husband's right-hands. The leader of the pack was Guillermo Perez-Santiago, who went by Gully. Jay's cousin and a former bounty hunter for the U.S. government, his glare was more intimidating than his muscles. Nevertheless, Kane would never let him know. The other two, Roman and Linx, stood so close, they rested on Kane's back.

Gully was the first to speak. "You get him, we'll be squared away."

The him he spoke of was an Afro-Cuban terrorist by the name of Ishmael Dumati. He not only killed Monifah and shot Jay, he also bombed a Brookstone city train and was attached to many attacks and murders in Kenema, Sierra Leone. He was at the top of every agency's Most Wanted List. If he was found alive, the prize was great. If he was found dead, the prize was even better. Or at least in Kane's opinion.

Gully offered his hand. Kane wasn't quick to take it until he saw Roman pick up his duffle bag. "All debts will be paid," Kane told him. He gave Gully's hand a firm shake. They had a longstanding beef, which started over a year ago when they met. Gully was Jay's cousin, which put him on Kane's bad side. Not that Gully's past with Jay was any better. Regardless of their familial problems, the proverb, blood is thicker than water, was a truth Gully lived by.

Carmen knew it as well. From her balcony, she watched to see what Gully was going to do. When him and Kane shook hands, it did more than soothe her nerves. It confirmed Gully was clueless to what she and Kane had done. She wanted her infidelity to follow her to the grave. With Kane's Jeep disappearing behind the front gate, her wish appeared to be granted. She also could move on to her next target.

Time for Lownes, Carmen thought. He was the only person standing in between her and Dumati. She left her balcony and headed down the steps. When she opened the front door, two familiar faces were staring back at her. *It can't be.* Their presence stole her breath. *It's not possible.* Shock prevented any sounds from leaving her mouth.

At her door, stood Lady and Hector Santiago—Jay's deceased parents.

TWO

Carmen walked backwards into the foyer. *They were murdered. They're dead. I know they're dead. This isn't real. I'm in some fucked up dream.* She pinched herself. *I felt that.* So many thoughts ran through her mind. For one, in the early nineties, the house she lived in was known as Casa de Sangre. Now, it was the Santiago Estate. It was the house her husband grew up in, which he inherited from his parents. His father, Hector Santiago, was close with hers, the late Lotus Pagua. Their relationship soured when her father broke away from the Santiago cartel. Hurt by the decision, Hector retaliated in one of the worst ways possible. He slept with her mother, Patricia, which resulted in the birth of her only sister, Eleise. The indiscretion gave her and Jay a shared sibling.

In addition to Casa de Sangre, Jay owned another house on the outskirts of East Brookstone. The house served as Jay's residence for most of his twenties until he sold it at the age of forty-nine. Various portraits of his parents decorated the living room. Carmen saw the photos every day when she lived there. The people in front of her was identical to them. Hector, who was full-blooded Taíno, had olive skin with dark chestnut brown hair. He didn't look anything like Jay, yet his blood gave her husband his caramel bronze complexion. Lady, on the other hand, had skin dipped in rich Godiva chocolate. Jay told her his mother could trace her roots to Africa, but he never told her which country. "It doesn't matter anyway," he would say. "She was born in Puerto Rico. She's Puerto Rican."

When Jay sold the property, the portraits were stored away, but the images were never forgotten. Now able to catch her breath, Carmen parted her lips only to be interrupted by shattering glass. The sound set off Jay's parents and one by one, they marched past her, yelling in Spanish. She turned around to find Gully with puddles of orange juice and broken glass at his feet.

"Mom," he croaked.

Carmen's heartbeat regulated. *These are Gully's parents?* They were now in his face, his father hitting him upside his head while his mother pulled his pants over his hips. She didn't have a clue what they were saying until the volume of their words sent Akaila running down the steps. Her daughter spoke fluent Spanish due to her Dominican/Puerto Rican background.

"They aren't happy about Jay," Akaila translated, "and his mother isn't happy that Gully is in his forties and still doesn't know how to wear a belt."

It all made sense. Gully's father was Hector's brother, which explained the resemblance. Why Gully's mother looked like Lady, Carmen didn't know, but when his mother pointed at her, she got an inkling an answer was coming.

"She said he'll never find a woman," Akaila continued, "if he can't dress."

Carmen walked up to them, not wanting to interrupt the family reunion, but to stop the chatter. She also wanted to save Gully from any conversation involving a woman. He wasn't open about his sexuality, but she knew from her husband, he was gay. "Hi, I'm Carmen." She stuck out her hand to his mother first.

"Señora Santiago." His mother didn't shake her hand. "Patricia's daughter, right?"

Carmen didn't want to admit she was. It *was* her mother who shot her sister-in-law after Lady discovered her affair with Hector. "I'm Jay's wife," she said instead.

"Guillermo! Señora!"

Silvas' voice boomed from the back of the foyer. Jay's butler was standing at his bedroom door with Rakim and Nyla. He put some pep in his step at the presence of Gully's parents. "It's been years. Look at you." He stepped over the spilled juice and greeted them with open arms.

Gully used the interruption to his advantage.

"Where did they come from?" Carmen asked after Gully pulled her in the dining room.

"I don't know. I ain't talked to them in years." Gully plopped down in a chair. He covered his face, still caught off guard. "Maybe they heard about Jay from the news. I dunno."

"Someone had to know they were coming. They got through the gate."

They met eyes.

"Cesar," they said in unison, referring to another one of Jay's right-hands.

Carmen joined him at the table. She looked in the foyer to see his parents hugging Rakim and Nyla. "Well, they're excited to see the kids." She turned her attention to Gully, this time noticing his trembling hands. "Talk to me." She grabbed his hands, yet his chance was stolen when Silvas' baritone filled the dining room.

"Oh, I'm gonna make a feast," Silvas exclaimed. "We'll have some mofongo. I got fresh pineapple for pina coladas. I'll make some fritters. Oh, y'all just chill out here. I'm gonna whip it up." He hurried in the kitchen while Guillermo and Señora joined them at the table.

Unsure of what to say, Carmen remained quiet. It worked to her benefit because her silence gave Gully's parents the floor. They answered her questions without her asking. Like Gully suggested, they learned about the shooting at The Ave on the news. The fear of losing their only nephew pricked the guilt in their hearts. "We disowned Jay when we found out he was selling drugs," Señora told her. "We had already gone through that with Hector." They contacted Cesar, which is how they learned Gully repaired his relationship with Jay. Their son became another reason for them to visit. Nevertheless, the nature of that relationship was never discussed. Nor did Carmen learn why they hadn't talked to their only son in years.

Food didn't stop the conversation either. Silvas kept his promise, preparing a lunch fit for royalty. Even with a full spread on the table, Gully's parents talked between bites. Despite not addressing the elephant in the room, they did share a major detail Carmen should've known prior to their arrival. Aunt Señora was not only Jay's aunt by marriage, but also his mother's sister. It further explained the resemblance to Lady along with the similarities in their names.

"I can help you with the kids while you see after Jay," Señora offered. "That's if you're fine with us staying for a few days."

Carmen liked the idea. The extra help would alleviate the baggage she'd put on Silvas and her maid, Fiona. Rakim and Nyla would also get a chance to learn more about their Puerto Rican heritage. Those were lessons she wanted to start early rather than later. After lunch, while Silvas rested from his feast, Carmen headed upstairs to clean one of the guestrooms. Once it was Mr. Clean-approved, she excused herself to meet Lownes. It left Rakim and Nyla in the care of Guillermo and Señora for the entire afternoon.

Lownes lived in a white ranch-style house between East and West Brookstone. Sanders hadn't given her his number, which meant her visit was like Gully's parents—unexpected. A Jeep Gladiator was in the driveway, a sign he was at home. Still, it took two knocks before he answered. His appearance caught her off guard, his attractiveness on the level of a Tyler Lepley. His model-like looks made her outline him from head to toe. It was her first mistake yet her first win. When her gaze shifted to his face, she was met with a fist, which she caught in her hand.

"Good reflex," he told her. "Never take your eyes off your target."

He turned away from her, walking further in the house. She followed behind him, closing the door behind her. "I heard you could help me," she said, joining him in his kitchen. A half-eaten hot dog was on a plate, a few empty beer bottles beside it.

"Have some?" He slid the hot dog towards her.

"Look, I don't have time for the shenanigans."

"You need me, right?" Lownes picked up the hot dog and stuffed it in his mouth. Despite his mouth being full, he kept talking. "What do you know about Dumati? You know more than the Triad?" He opened his fridge and took out another beer. "What about the CIA? The FBI? They're all gunning for this man. Kane didn't tell you that, did he?"

"I don't know a lot," she admitted.

"So, don't bring the shenanigans to me." He popped the cap off the bottle. "I used to work for the Triad," he continued. "I left when I got an offer from another agency to investigate them. Someone planted a fake diamond."

That someone was her ex-husband, Kane. Years ago, she stole the Pink Sunrise diamond from her then-boyfriend, Jay, who stole it from a private collector. To get her out a prison sentence, Kane planted a fake in Jay's house, reported he found the Pink Sunrise, only for it to test as a cubic zirconia. Carmen was released from prison although the real diamond was in her possession.

Kane was put on leave from the Triad, but it wasn't because of the Pink Sunrise. He was put on leave because of their relationship. While Kane was investigating Jay for drug trafficking, he was also courting her. That courtship turned into a marriage months after her prison release.

"I protected him," Lownes dispelled. "That's why he didn't go down for it. We started at the Training Academy together. I bet you didn't know I was his partner on that case. I know about you, Mrs. Santiago. I've been watching you since you were twenty-one."

"Sanders sent me to you."

Lownes set the bottle on the counter after a long swig. "He knows something the Triad doesn't." He walked past her into his living room. He returned with a laptop, which he opened on the counter. "I'm a triple agent. That means I know what three different agencies know. Also, what they don't want each other to know." He typed a bit on his laptop before turning the screen towards her. He was in a program called MXP. He did a search for Ishmael Dumati, which turned his screen black and populated numerous windows. With one click of the mouse, the windows became frozen in a block formation, creating a criminal profile.

"Everyone knows he's off the grid," he continued. "What everyone doesn't know is his ties to this man." Lownes clicked on the name Alejandro Salazar, which took him to another profile. A picture loaded of an older Hispanic gentleman. "He was one of the biggest drug lords in Cuba. He was arrested in the early nineties for smuggling cocaine and heroin into the U.S.

He got out, opened a few businesses, but there's no evidence of drug trafficking."

"If they're associates, he's still in the game."

"That's why we think he's Dumati's plug," Lownes shared. "We just can't prove it."

"Do you know where he is? You said he's a businessman."

Lownes smiled. "He's living in the Entertainment Capital of the World."

Las Vegas was a city that was no stranger to her. From the nightlife to the city's fine dining establishments, Vegas' bright lights was the reason people around the world flocked to Nevada. Once upon a time, she was one of them. It was part of the reason she told Lownes she would fly there to find Salazar. She accepted the task although she didn't know how she would complete it. Even with Gully's parents in town, her village was stretched thin.

Or so she thought. When she arrived home, she shared her plans with Silvas and Fiona. The two were the reason her house stayed on the right side of the ground. They were also surrogate grandparents to her kids.

"I want to sit with Jay," Silvas expressed. "I'll take care of him."

"I'm glad you're leaving," Fiona voiced. "Now I can have my babies to myself." The babies, in this instance, were Rakim and Nyla.

There went a laugh Carmen didn't know she needed. "They're yours," she joked. "You only have to share them with Guillermo and Señora." Rakim and Nyla were sitting with Gully's parents at the dining room table. Señora was showing them a map of Puerto Rico, sharing stories about their family's life on the island.

Carmen didn't deliver the news of her trip to her youngest two until she tucked them in. They both were in Rakim's bed, the sleeping arrangement serving as a coping mechanism to help them deal with Jay's condition.

"Will we be able to call you?" Nyla asked.

Carmen kissed her cheek. "No, you won't, but I'm gonna call you. I will tell you this," she grabbed their hands in hers, "I'm gonna be thinking about y'all every second."

"Is Fiona gonna take us to see Daddy?" Rakim spoke up this time.

Carmen stared into her son's hazel eyes. "Every day," she replied.

This time, she planted a kiss on both their hands. The same affection was given to Bella once she was at the hospital. For the past two or so hours, they bonded for the first time through skin-to-skin. Not only was it healthy for the baby, it was the perfect gift for Carmen before her trip. If only she could get the same warmth from Jay.

"I know this isn't something you want me to do," she told him, now in his room. "I can hear you telling me to leave it alone. I can't, though. I need to do this for our family." She ran her fingers through his curls. "I wish I could tell you how this was going to end."

She told herself not to cry. Almost nightly, his hospital gown had been catching her tears. It didn't need any more. The journey she was embarking on needed a traveler who was confident in their ability. It wasn't worth leaving his side if she didn't have a sense of her strength. Therefore, not one tear was shed. She left the room with only the words, *I love you*, in his ear. While she didn't know it then, he left her with a gift of his own, a flicker of his eyes.

THREE

The bright sunny skies of Miami were an instant reminder to Kane he was no longer in New York. Long gone were freezing winds, snowstorms, and slippery ice. Clear and present were palm trees, ocean waves, and bikini-clad women. Or at least that was the scenery in South Beach. His visual now was cruise and cargo ships. Known as the cruise capital of the world, the Port of Miami also held a Triad autoliner, TR SOBE. The name painted on the vessel, though, was Amara.

The carrier was primarily used to transport vehicles for undercover operations. It was uncommon for any agent to use it for travel. After this case, it wouldn't be. The current captain of the Triad, Paul Donahue, requested the new travel arrangement. With many pending investigations, the Triad was on a strict budget. Kane's operation was on an even stricter budget. By having him travel to Jamaica on the same ship as the Cadillac Escalade they gave him, it minimized flight costs.

Kane agreed to the plan and now he was showing various forms of ID to Florida's resident Triad agents. Once he was granted clearance, he drove the SUV onto the vessel's West ramp. His fellow agents secured it in a parking space where it would stay for the next two days. Another security check followed, which granted him access to his living quarters. While he didn't expect a five-star accommodation, he thought he would have a room he could do more than sleep in.

That's all they want me to do, he thought, sliding his duffle bag underneath the bed. He understood why, too. Once his foot hit Jamaican soil, it was on.

***

Salazar had numerous businesses in the Las Vegas area. A car dealership, restaurants, cigar lounges, and several boutique stores were attached to his name. However, there was only one Lownes wanted Carmen to focus on. La Zona Roja or The Red Zone, was a five-star gentleman's club located right off The Strip. Salazar was regularly photographed outside it, which meant it was a business he frequented.

"You're a woman," Lownes told her. "Figure out how to get his attention."

"I'm a woman, but I'm competing with that." She pointed at his laptop's screen. In the video that was playing, a half-naked, racially ambiguous woman dangled off a stripper pole. "I also gave birth to four kids. It shows in these curves."

"Your curves are natural," Lownes countered. "I didn't say you have to strip. I said get his attention. If he's there, make yourself known. You can wipe your ass with all the money you got. Throw them chicks some. Everyone will be on your ass if you're a heavy tipper. You may catch his eye because you caught someone else's."

Carmen could admit he had a point. *Sapphire prepared me for this.* She reminisced about her days at Jay's club. Due to the leadership of her husband, the venue had become one of New York's top-rated establishments. The who's who of the world flocked to the club just to be photographed inside its walls. Sapphire was known for its saturated shade of blue while La Zona Roja was patterned after red.

"That's how you got Kane, right?"

Her mind had been elsewhere. She hadn't caught what Lownes said. "What?"

"You caught his eye because you caught Jay's."

Carmen shrugged her shoulders. "Perhaps," was all she gave him. She could've said more, but more would've sent her down a rabbit hole. Lownes knew the story anyway. He told her at their first meeting he was Kane's partner and had been following her since she was twenty-one.

"Did you really love him?"

The word, "what," sounded out her mouth again. She didn't know if he was asking about Jay or Kane. Either way it went, the answer was yes. In the end, though, Santiago would be the name she died with. About to express it, an incoming call kept her from doing so. Gomez, Jay's lawyer, hit her line, which was a call she had to take. She excused herself from Lownes.

"I'm glad we could touch base," she greeted. She stood in a hallway a few feet from Lownes' living room.

"I've been meaning to reach out to you," Gomez said. "You know I've been praying for Jay."

"Keep the prayers going," she replied. "Did you listen to my message?"

"I did," he said. Silence entered the line, but it was brief. "I didn't help Jay with his will. That's not my area of expertise. However, I do have a copy of it. I also have a copy of the agreement I signed which says I can't disclose any details of the will until he's declared dead. What I can tell you is that he did right by you and the kids. You don't have anything to worry about."

"That's all I wanted to know."

"Believe it or not," Gomez told her, "in the end, you'll know more than me. If anything happens to him, the entire Santiago dynasty is in your hands. I have the key, but once you take it, you unlock the door."

"Hopefully, that won't happen."

The sound of footsteps took her attention away from the call. Lownes joined her in the hall. At the sight of him, she thanked Gomez for his time and hung up. "What's the budget for this thing?" She hoped to steer his mind back to Salazar.

The question gave him a chuckle. "Whatever is in your checking account."

***

The moment the Escalade rolled off the West ramp, Kane was met with the blazing rays of Jamaica's morning sun. The sight of it took him back to the first time he visited the island. He was a newlywed with two young children at home. Carmen didn't want him to take the assignment because of it. Against her wishes, he did, using the monetary incentives as an excuse. If he stood in his truth, he would've admitted he accepted the case because of his desire for the role.

A large part of his childhood was spent watching *Scarface*. The lifestyle of Tony Montana enticed him. It was unlike his actual reality, which was a traditional Christian middle class household. In high school, he was known as the nice guy and was never feared or tested. Girls weren't fanning over him as he was usually their second choice after the dope boys and Al B. Sure-looking dudes ran through them. That was why getting Carmen was a win. He was able to catch her eye despite not being a Tony Montana. Then, the Triad gave him the opportunity to become him. His assignment was to pose as a drug dealer to take down Jamaica's biggest drug lord, Luck Myers.

Upon arriving in Jamaica, King Kong was born. Kong was a dark knight, who came to Kingston out of nowhere with a shitload of money and the best cocaine the island had ever seen. The operation's budget allowed him to rent a luxury home, further creating the aesthetic of a kingpin. A multi-million dollar property, his house had women dropping their panties at the door. Those antics led his team to create a don't ask, don't tell policy. What happened in Kingston, stayed in Kingston. His presence soon caught the eye of Luck as he was fresh competition. Luck handled it differently than most. He befriended him. To further earn Luck's trust, Kane shut down his operation and joined Luck's.

Within weeks, he was monitoring Luck's trafficking routes. He had enough knowledge and wiretaps of Luck's operation to set up a raid. He delayed it for a month because he wasn't ready to let go of Kong. He feared losing the key to life—money, power, and respect. Still, a decision had to be made. The realization hit him when he committed his fifth murder on the island. He was lost in the world of Kong.

Three days later, he was in the basement of the island's Triad office, putting on a bulletproof vest and a black tactical mask. Guns in hand, he ran inside Luck's house with fifty other agents. Eighteen years had passed since that day. Luck was now buried in May Pen Cemetery, having died eight years earlier from stomach cancer. It was always Kane's plan to have a conversation with him, but he was too consumed with life to walk into a fake one of the past.

Now, he was driving into it. Miles away from the Kingston Harbour, he turned up the stereo's volume. Cutty Ranks, "Limb by Limb," breathed life into Kong, swallowing any remains of Michael Kane. He rolled the windows down, desperate to attract any attention he could. He needed people to see him even if they didn't know who he was. Word needed to get out about the Escalade with the New York plate.

He didn't know if it did when he approached a group of armed men at the gate of the Parish Estate. The home was the residence of Presi, a former capo in Myers' cartel. The name Presi, a play on the word President, was given to the capo by Luck due to the number of businesses he owned. Their paths crossed on the daily until he arrested Presi with the rest of Luck's cartel. It was a dangerous feat to approach him, but Presi was a potential lifeline to Dumati.

The Escalade came to a rolling stop in front of four men whose complexions matched his own. To show them the visit was pleasant, Kane turned off the engine and unlocked the doors. He held up both hands as if law enforcement were stopping him. One by one each of his doors was opened. Four machine guns entered his vehicle, the barrel of one now resting on his temple.

Kane was quick with his request. "Kong to see Presi."

"Who?" the man said to his left. "Wi kno no Kong."

"Kong to see Presi," he repeated.

He waited, knowing Presi was listening in. Then, he heard movement in his backseat. The doors closed and the barrel was lifted off his temple.

"Straight ahead." The man motioned with his gun.

Kane gave him a single head nod. He closed his door back, locking it, and drove through the gate. The ease of getting inside told him two things. One, Presi remembered him, and two, he wanted to see him. In terms of what was going to happen once he got behind closed doors, that was a different story.

The Parish Estate was a prime example of the success Presi had seen upon his release. The exterior of the mansion was outfitted with all-white architecture. An exquisite angel fountain had been constructed in the middle of the estate's driveway creating a lane for arrivals and departures. If that wasn't enough, three luxury vehicles were parked in front of the home. Kane's would be the fourth. He stepped out the Escalade, catching a glimpse of himself in the rearview mirror. Everything about his appearance screamed Kong. From the two-carat diamond gold stud in his left ear to the diamond chain around his neck. Neither was something he wore back in Brookstone.

"Walk," a man said behind him. He didn't have a Jamaican accent.

Kane felt the barrel of a gun in his back. The man's frame was in a blind spot, which kept him from seeing his reflection in his side rearview mirror. Not that it mattered. He was on Presi's turf, which meant he played by his rules. He followed the directive until he was face to face with Presi in his living room. With the opportunity there, he looked behind him. Automatically, he sucked his teeth. Everything about the man's features screamed Jay—light skin, hazel-green colored eyes. He hated him from that moment because he reminded him of Carmen's husband.

Presi spoke. "Tek a seat."

Presi saw his eyes on the man. If he hadn't said something, Kane would've continued to stare him down. He would've even cursed him. Instead of doing what he wanted to do, Kane did what he needed to do. He sat across from Presi who was watching an episode of *Golden Girls*.

"Yuh a dead man walking," Presi told him.

Kane agreed. "I've been that for eighteen years."

"Yuh let Luck die in there."

Kane was aware of what he'd done. "Which is why I'm here to right my wrongs."

Presi made a confession. "I know who yuh are."

Kane looked across the room at the Jay look-a-like. Presi caught the glance as well.

"Gi wi sum privacy," Presi said to the man.

The man hesitated in leaving, but eventually left the room. In the meantime, Kane took a moment to examine Presi. The man's age showed in his face. Kane suspected him to be somewhere in his sixties. Although he wanted to reminisce about their better days, he put an apology on the table. "What I did wasn't an easy thing to do. I created a bond with you. Yes, it started out as a lie, but it became real. I had your back in some shit. You gotta remember that."

"But nuh weh it matta."

His accent still thick as hell. Kane repeated Presi's words in his head until he caught on to what he said. *But not where it mattered.* "I'm sorry for what I did to you and Luck. I'm sorry for what I did to us. At one point, I was sincere, but it was still a job. I played my part and got my check."

"Mi wa fin' to kill yuh."

"You would've done that if you wanted to." Kane spoke truth. "There were five opportunities. Four of them met me at the gate."

"Yuh worth more alive dan dead."

Those words told Kane something he didn't know. He was there for a request, but Presi had one of his own. What he was going to ask of him, he didn't know. What he did know was that it kept a bullet out his ass.

"Wah do yuh want?" Presi asked.

"Have you heard of Ishmael Dumati?"

Presi changed his position in his seat. "Mi hear di name once."

"Can you tell me who said it to you?"

Presi looked him in the eye. "Fi a price."

Kane shook his head. "You know I ain't got shit. You said you know who I am."

"Di investigation. Make it go away."

Presi's request made Kane narrow his eyes. He didn't know there was an investigation. It wasn't mentioned in Presi's criminal profile, which he reviewed to find his address. "Who's investigating you? It ain't us. I just looked at your shit."

Presi didn't answer the question. "Make it go away."

"You're telling me to find out." It was never Kane's intention to stop by the Triad office in Kingston. While they were all one team, things got rocky when you stepped on another office's turf. If the Kingston Triad were investigating Presi, they would have to halt the operation until Dumati was found. Besides, capturing Dumati was a bigger payday than Presi. The U.S. government was expected to drop at least a billion in their hands if Dumati was found. "I owe you this one," Kane continued. "I can't make anything up to Luck, but I can square things away with you. I'll find out what's going on and end it."

Presi pointed towards the ceiling. Kane followed his finger until his eyes landed on a camera. He was recording their conversation. "I'll make it go away," Kane said to him. "Consider it done. All I need is that name. Shit, you got me now. You can send this tape right to the Triad."

"I wi have more." Presi pressed the face of his watch. "Brick," he said into it.

In that instant, the door to the living room opened. The Jay look-a-like, who Kane now knew as Brick, came inside. It was obvious he'd been eavesdropping.

"Get di suitcases," Presi ordered.

Brick followed the command, leaving the room. Kane used the privacy to his advantage. "Can I have that name?"

"Salazar," Presi replied. "Alejandro Salazar."

Kane's eyes widened. Why he didn't put two and two together he didn't know. His mistake was a rookie one. Dumati was Afro-Cuban. If anything, he should've known his plug was the man who was once considered Cuba's biggest drug lord.

"Both dem guh to him," Presi told him.

Brick was back in the room. A black suitcase in each of his hands.

"To Salazar?" Kane asked. He looked back and forth between Brick and Presi.

"Deliva it tuh him."

Presi motioned to Brick. The gesture sent Kane's eyes back to the suitcases. Brick opened each one showing him the stacks of crisp bills. The money told him two things. Not only was Salazar the plug, Presi was still in the drug game. By having him deliver the money to Salazar, Presi was putting him on his team. He would also have the transaction recorded.

"He goes wid yuh," Presi ordered.

That was an order Kane didn't want. If he couldn't stand the sight of Jay, he wasn't going to stand the sight of Brick. There went something else he had to take for the team. "Consider it delivered," he told him. "Where do I find him?"

Presi changed positions again before clearing his throat. "Las Vegas."

FOUR

Silvas' fingers were wrapped around the handles of his travel tote as if it were about to fly out the car. Carmen told him to put it in the backseat, but he preferred to have it in his lap. "I appreciate you doing this," Carmen expressed. "I know you consider Jay your son, but you don't have to give up your time like this. That room can get lonely when no one is talking back to you."

"All that matters is that he's alive," Silvas responded.

"That's what I tell myself." Carmen pulled in front of the entrance of the hospital. She drove herself as there were a slew of things she needed to do before she boarded a flight to Vegas. She looked in her rearview mirror to see who was behind her. Typically, Lia, another one of her husband's right-hands, would be trailing her. While she expected to see Lia's black car, Carmen got King and Malachi. Her eldest was walking towards her, giving the impression he was bothered. "I know you don't do drama," she said to Silvas, unlocking the doors. "So, you may wanna head inside."

Silvas placed his hand on hers. "You know how to take care of yourself. Come back to Jay so he can come back to you." He got out the car right as King opened her door.

"Oh, you know you about to get it," her son yelled.

Carmen laughed in his face. "Am I the parent or are you?"

"You tell me. I ain't tryin' to run to Vegas. You got three fuckin' kids to see about." He spoke specifically of the youngest three, Rakim, Nyla, and Bella.

The f-bomb made Carmen step out her car. She figured either Kristian or Akaila had told him about her trip to Sin City. "Look, I know you think you're grown because you're a husband and all, but chu ain't gonna talk to me like that. I was in the streets before you. I got this."

"Mama, these ain't no corner boys you're tryin' to go after. These are Escobar, Mafia-type muthafuckas."

"You mean Jay Santiago-type muthafuckas?" She glanced at Malachi who was at his side. He grinned at her response. "Rakim and Nyla got five people at the house watching them. Matter of fact, y'all need to come over for dinner so you can meet your aunt and uncle. They came up from Bayamon. Oh, and guess what surprise Kane left for me? His parents are moving into his condo to help with Bella. So, those three kids you're concerned about? Your mama is leaving them with a stable village."

"You're too old for this," King shot back.

"There ain't an age limit on asking a question."

King was huffing and puffing like she told him he couldn't have a Tonka truck. "You need to at least take Linx with you. I got Coco and Prince now," he said, speaking of his wife and son, "I can't be out there like that. I wanna get this son of a bitch, too, but I'm gonna let Kane handle it."

"No one is coming with me."

The tension was leaving King's body, but not as quickly as she wanted it to. Therefore, she did the one thing she knew would calm him. She grabbed him in her arms, resting him against her bosom. "You were with me for two months before I knew you were there," she whispered. "I was pregnant, selling drugs, shit, I committed a murder. I can handle whatever is out there. If I can't, I'll come home. Is that a deal?"

"He tried to take my dad," King cried. "I can't lose you."

Carmen understood his fear. Jay had only been in his life for the past four years. For the first seventeen years of his life, she led him to believe Kane was his biological father. He learned the truth upon Jay's release from prison. While his relationship with Jay had its highs and lows, King loved the hell out of him. "You're not gonna lose us. Jay is in the hospital fightin' and I'm gonna be out here fightin'. We love you." She kissed his cheek. "Go see your father. He needs to feel your energy."

When King relaxed in her arms, she knew they were good. She released her hold only to turn towards Malachi. After a lengthy embrace, they all parted ways. King and Malachi went inside the hospital while Carmen's next stop was Verizon to buy a cell phone for Rakim and Nyla. The purchase was one she would've discussed with Jay, but the odds were against them. In the event she couldn't reach anyone, she needed another way to see and speak to her kids.

After she left the store, she went to Cricket, as suggested by Lownes, and bought a burner phone. She didn't know who or what she was about to meet in Vegas. All she knew is that once she left the city, if needed, no one there would be able to contact her again.

Speaking of Sin City, she thought to herself. She was now standing inside a local lingerie store. She'd seen enough in Sapphire and in YouTube videos of La Zona Roja to know she had to match the culture. There were sexy clothes in her closet, but it wasn't the sexy she needed. She had couture sexy. She needed hardcore sexy. The type of sexy that made jaws drops and dicks get hard. Lownes stressed that to catch Salazar she needed to catch an eye. If it meant playing dress up for a night or two, she could do it. Once she caught that eye, though, she wanted Salazar on a platter.

***

With DMX's, "Top Shotter," blasting through his speakers, Kane drove the Escalade onto the aviation ramp. One hand was on the wheel, the other dialed Sanders' number. When he didn't hear it ringing, he cut the extra noise. Three seconds later, Sanders was saying hello.

"I gotta get another car," Kane told him. "Tell Donahue I have to do it."

"Did you fuck up the Escalade?" Sanders' words came out like a shriek.

"Nah, but I can't drive the shit through the ocean. Presi gave me a lead, but it's in Vegas. The only thing that saved my ass is that he's letting me fly there on his private jet. I can't leave the Escalade in Kingston. You know what's in it. I've already called the Triad office here. An agent is gonna pick it up and put it on the auto liner headed to LA. One of the Cali agents can drive it to me after it hits the coast."

"What happened with Presi? How are you going from Kingston to Vegas in one day?"

"Look, I can't say much. I'm still figuring it out," he lied. The truth was that there was nothing to figure out. Only things to hide. One of those things was that Presi was still a drug dealer. If Presi wanted him to stop an investigation, he couldn't incriminate him by sharing too many details. He would've told Sanders the truth if the Triad didn't tap his lines. Unfortunately, his former partner wasn't smart enough to get a burner phone. "Just let Donahue know I'm using the card. I gotta have the baddest shit, too."

"What's the lead in Vegas?"

"I gotta board the plane," Kane said, seeing Brick. "I'll call you once I land."

***

It felt weird to be stepping inside Caesars Palace for a reason that had nothing to do with fashion. Carmen's hotel of choice whenever she visited Las Vegas, she knew it like the back of her hand. What didn't feel weird was the aura of Hollywood glamour that hit her when she walked through the doors. Even now, she indulged in the ambience of the Roman fantasyland.

Unfortunately, the moment was fleeting. The second someone stepped in her view, she got the reminder of why she was there. Nothing about the trip was a vacation. That meant she needed to get moving. Having boarded an evening flight, she had enough time to get changed and get to La Zona Roja before the club closed.

Another first for her was that she hadn't booked a villa. In the earlier stages of her career, the Claudius Villa was the place she and Kane would call home. They only had King and Kristian at the time, which meant the kids could have their own room even on a "work vacation." The current trip didn't require such luxury. Therefore, she booked a room in the hotel's Augustus Tower. It was still more room than she needed, but when you had money, you could live like it.

She also wanted to look like it. The dress she chose for the night was a cyber yellow leather mini. The top of the dress was balconette which made her cleavage give a big hello to anyone who crossed its path. The dress fit every inch of her curves showing off her defined waistline. If Jay were to see her in it, he would've had it at her ankles.

Damn, I want you so bad.

The memory of their sexcapades had to hold her. If Kane had cooperated, she wouldn't have been so bad off. She still couldn't believe he denied her. For most of their marriage, although requested, she never went down on him. Now that she wanted to do it, he didn't let her. She understood why, though. Their relationship wasn't going anywhere. The breath in Jay's lungs made that clear.

What wasn't clear was what she was going to do inside La Zona Roja. She paid the fifty dollar cover charge and was now standing in a large room known as The Angels Cabaret. The entire space was outfitted in crimson red from the lightning fixtures around the performance areas to the leather armchairs and tables along the rail of the stage. Circular crimson red couches were in each corner of the room along with a stripper pole. Mostly men occupied those areas where one or two dancers entertained them. She watched for a bit, admiring the talent, until she was violated.

The hand palmed her ass so quick, Carmen had to think twice if it occurred. She looked behind her to catch a girl's eyes locked on hers. The buxom beauty was headed to the back of the club. While Carmen had only seen her for a second, she saw enough. The girl's body could've landed her in the pages of *KING* magazine. Soft jet black curls floated down her back while her face was the perfect mix of Erica Mena and Alexa Demie. She donned a black mesh bodysuit, but was braless underneath, giving everyone a peek at her large, perky breasts. Her lower region was covered by a red leopard-print wrap. Unsure of why she touched her, Carmen wasn't going to follow her to find out. If anything, she was going to stay out her way.

That was the reason she headed to the bar. Several people were waiting to order, so it took a moment before a bartender approached her. She was dressed like the girl who palmed her ass. However, her nipples were covered by red sequined pasties. *Don't let it faze you. You're at a gentleman's club in Vegas.* "Can I have a Manhattan?" The bartender's mouth dropped open like she was taken aback at the request.

"I know you," the bartender squealed.

Carmen was now the one taken aback. In fact, she stepped back. "You know me?"

"You're, you're, I've seen you on magazines. You're Car—"

"Karma," Carmen said. The name came out of nowhere. "Karma Levy."

"Karma," the bartender repeated. "Yes, that's it, Karma."

Carmen smiled at how easily she swayed her. "How about that Manhattan?"

"Right, I'm on it."

When she left to prepare the drink, Carmen turned away. Her eyes went to the main stage where a girl was performing. Mounds of cash covered the stage, the visual reminding her of the time she and Jay sexed on his money. Duffle bags of hundred dollar bills were dumped on her, the money serving as an aphrodisiac.

"Here you go," she heard the bartender call.

Carmen turned around to find the bartender handing her the drink. Meanwhile, the girl from earlier approached the bar. Carmen didn't make eye contact with her, wanting to let the whole thing go. If she was a man, she would've handled it differently although either way was a violation.

"It's fifteen," the bartender stated. "Do you want to start a tab?"

"Nah, this will probably be it for the night." Carmen reached into her clutch and pulled out a fifty dollar bill. "Keep the change." She turned away, now trying to scope out a place to sit. When she spotted an empty chair towards the back of the room, she headed to it. Still in earshot, she overhead what the bartender said to the girl.

"That's big money right there. Go get it."

Now, why are you setting her up to get slapped? Carmen kept walking, rolling her eyes at the same time. She stopped, when once again, she remembered where she was. If the girl was a dancer, it was her job to go where the money was. *It ain't like she knows I'm not here to be entertained.*

Once seated, Carmen's eyes traveled all over the club. Her lips never touched her drink. When that got old, she pulled out the burner phone. She sent a text to Lownes, *Roja*, letting him know she was there. While she waited for a response, she did a Google search of the phrase *Angels Cabaret Las Vegas*.

Most of the websites that came up were links where patrons had reviewed the club or belonged to other strip clubs in the area. On the third page, she found a message board post on *Lipstick Alley*. *The Cabaret, An Angels' Whorehouse*, was the headline. Already intrigued, Carmen read the post, detailing what appeared to be an escort service disguised as a gentleman's club. A girl, under the username, caramel_dollaz, wrote the post, describing how she was invited by a stripper at La Zona Roja to attend a party at a huge Las Vegas mansion.

It was some birthday party for the club's owner. Loads of people were there, all dressed like they had money. When I got inside, they took my cell phone and purse. They put it in this room and told me I would get it back when I left. I was like, whatever, and was led by this skinny blonde chick downstairs. Turns out it was some fuckin' orgy party. Men were watching girls eat each other out. There were even a few dudes in the room getting their dicks sucked. When I saw a girl take a hundred dollar bill from this dude, I was outta there. I got my purse and dipped. On the way out, I spotted Jas, she was the one who invited me. She's this Puerto Rican chick from the Bay. She's like one of the main hoes. I was like, what the fuck is this shit?

She told me she invited me because I told her at the club about my tuition issues. I was like, yeah, I'm broke as hell, but I ain't about to sell no pussy. She was like, nah, it ain't that, we just have fun or whatever, and get money. Yeah, bish, get money by sellin' your pussy. The owner, some Cuban dude, told me to get my ass off his property. He didn't have to tell me twice. I'm telling y'all, if you see this girl, run. She will try to whore you out!

Carmen scrolled down the post to find a picture of Jas. The image made her raise a brow as she put two and two together. Jas was the girl who palmed her ass.

I bet you took one look at me and wanted to make me a recruit.

"You missed my dance."

Carmen dropped her phone at the sight of Jas. The girl had changed out the black mesh bodysuit but wasn't in anything much different. Her new suit was made completely of black lace, her naked breasts still on full display. Not responding, Carmen picked up her phone, glad it fell with the screen down. "It wasn't personal," she told her once her phone was in her hands. "I'll catch the next one." She slipped her phone inside her clutch.

"You mean the one right now?"

It was on the tip of Carmen's tongue to tell her to get the fuck out her face until Lownes' voice sounded in her head. *You may catch his eye because you caught someone else's.* There she was, trying to push Jas away when she needed her. She knew from the message board post that Jas was an escort for Salazar. It was now her job to befriend her. *No, it's Karma's,* she reminded herself.

She reached inside her clutch and pulled out a fifty dollar bill. *I can't believe I'm about to do this.* She slipped it inside the left shoulder strap of Jas' bodysuit. "Whatever that will give me."

Jas laughed in her face. "Why did you come here? You're sitting up here on your phone like you're bored as hell. Who does that at a club? Who does that at *this* club?"

Carmen didn't let the questions faze her. "Are you gonna give me what I paid for?"

Jas slid on top of her lap. Carmen had never been that close to a woman. There was never a desire for it despite seeing women in all shapes and forms due to the nature of her business. As the CEO and head fashion designer of Flame, Inc., she had to find women attractive to book them for her ad campaigns. The buck stopped there, though.

"You like that?" Jas asked in her ear. She was gyrating, her crotch not hitting much due to Carmen's position in the chair and the fabric of her dress. Her moves were good, but better suited on someone other than her. Carmen memorized a few of them, planning to perform them on Jay once he was awake. "You like it," Jas continued.

Carmen gripped the sides of the chair to prevent herself from laughing. She was trying to be Karma Levy, the persona she created, but the whole thing was an epic fail. The Karma she envisioned in her head would like it. She would be so into it; she would ask to move to a VIP room. *That's what you should do,* a voice said in her head. *Don't chu want Salazar? You know she's the key to him. She can walk you up to his front door.* Carmen swallowed. "Can I touch you?" she asked.

"Now you know the reason I touched you," Jas whispered back.

Her response confirmed she was on Jas' radar. Carmen gripped the side of Jas' hip, holding her in place. "This is too public for me."

Jas scooted off her lap, putting space between them. "Fifty is what keeps you here."

It was obvious what that meant. Fifty kept her there, more gave her privacy. It worked to Jas' benefit that Carmen's money was long. To show her, Carmen reached inside her clutch. She pulled out three hundred dollar bills. The money made a smile appear on Jas' face. For the first time, Carmen saw her in a different light. Karma had taken over. She slid the money in the other strap of the bodysuit. "I go where you go."

Those words led her down a long hallway and into a barely lit room. One red leather sofa was inside along with a stripper pole. Jas locked the door the moment they were inside. Carmen expected her to straddle her again, which she did, but not until after Jas had the ends of her dress at her waist. Carmen didn't bother to pull it back down, instead, she spread her legs.

"Have you ever been with a woman?"

The word, no, rolled off Carmen's tongue. While they were in a sexual position, she didn't think she would be with one now. That was until Jas kissed her lips. It was a different sensation than what she was used to. Rough and aggressive is what Jay gave. Kane's kisses were softer, though nothing like Jas'. A part of her liked it. It was delicate and sensual at the same time.

Jas tested her, slipping her tongue inside her mouth. When Carmen returned the gesture, the gyrations started. The feel of her crotch against hers reminded her of what she'd done with Kane in her garage. All they did was hump each other since there wasn't any penetration. The act left them realizing how much they loved each other. She wasn't expecting to magically fall in love with Jas as that would never happen, but she became open to the experience.

They removed whatever fabric or panty was separating them aside and rubbed their clits against each other. The wetness made Carmen grind against her harder until she came right there on the couch. Jas exploded a few seconds later, her body completely naked on top of hers.

Carmen smiled, or rather, Karma smiled. Carmen was too distraught to do anything. Karma, on the other hand, didn't want it to end. Matter of fact, she couldn't let it. She pulled more bills from her purse. "Where else can we go?" She rubbed the bills against Jas' left nipple.

Jas smiled. "I can take you to heaven."

FIVE

Salazar's mansion was known as The Angels Paradise. From the moment her Uber pulled in front of the property, Carmen could see how the estate got its name. Windmill palm trees decorated the outskirts of the mansion while Roman and Caribbean-modeled luxury pools were on both sides of the estate. Paradise was an understatement. Like La Zona Roja, red was the home's color scheme. In the foyer, Carmen's elektra-blue pumps walked upon coral red marble flooring. Multiple porcelain white pillars stood on each side of the foyer, adding a taste of Roman architecture.

Every bit of it was camera-worthy, but nothing was as breathtaking as the portrait in the center right wall of the room. One she knew well, Carmen stood in front of it as if she was looking in a mirror. *Carmen of the Opera* was a piece she'd seen first as a child. The oil painting, completed by Barbara Weber, was based off the character, Carmen, in an opera of the same name. The portrait intrigued her although she'd never invested in a copy of it.

Jas interrupted her daze. "She looks like me, doesn't she?"

The painting was of a Spanish gypsy, so while Carmen thought of herself when she saw it, the woman looked more like Jas than her. "That's why I can't stop staring at her," she lied.

"It doesn't matter where you are in the room. Her eyes are always on you."

"Hmm, let's see." Carmen moved away from the painting, heading towards the foyer. When she reached the stairwell, Jas took the lead, showing her to the master suite. She pointed at a door. "That's the bathroom. You can freshen up in there. My boss will be home a little later."

"Perfect," Carmen replied. One of her suitcases was in her hand, which was filled with an assortment of items. She headed to the bathroom and went inside.

"I'll be back in a minute," Carmen heard behind her. "I'm going down the hall. If you hear voices, it's probably some of the girls coming home."

"Cool," was all Carmen said. She turned the light on in the bathroom, seeing it was also constructed for a king. Once Jas was out of earshot, she closed the door. She leaned against it, sliding down to the floor. The tears were coming fast. It was one thing to cheat on Jay with her ex-husband, it was another to do it with a girl she hadn't known for thirty minutes.

Jas looked like she was only a couple of years older than her daughters. *It got you where you needed to be,* a voice said in her head. *Shut up, stop bitchin', and play the game. You want Salazar, right? He's the ticket to Dumati. Get up and do what you need to do.*

Carmen wiped her face. She then opened her suitcase, starting her transformation into Karma. Twenty or so minutes later, she and Jas were on top of the bed. Salazar hadn't arrived, but the house wasn't as quiet as it was before. She could hear females talking outside the bedroom, although none of them ventured inside.

"I can't believe this was your first experience," Jas whispered. "You let a sexy lesbian turn you out."

Carmen was now dressed in a short black lace chemise. The dress had open cups, which she wore without nipple covers. Jas took advantage, sucking on her nipples while her fingers explored Pandora's Box. Carmen was about to return the favor when the door opened.

The sound took Jas' lips off her breast. "She's beautiful, isn't she?"

Salazar shot a quick glance Carmen's way. He looked like the picture she saw, his features reminding her of Lucky Luciano. He yelled a few words in Spanish as he undid the first two buttons on his shirt. Unsure if he was angry about her being there, Carmen sat up. Salazar didn't say anything else, going inside his closet. He moved a few things around but emerged empty-handed.

"Presi's men are downstairs. Get her ready," he ordered.

"She's for me," Jas told him. To confirm it, Jas slid her knee up towards Carmen's crotch. She gave her clit a soft rub. "Wanna watch us have fun?"

Salazar wasn't interested. "She's for them. All pussy is for them. Especially Black pussy."

Carmen raised up, but Jas pinned her back down. "Don't," Jas said in a firm tone. "That's not what he meant." She kissed her lips to calm her. "Presi's men are Jamaican."

Salazar headed towards the door. "I'll give you a minute to review the rules."

Carmen's chest heaved. This was the moment she told King about. If things went too far, she would come home. She was about to be on the next flight to Brookstone.

"Act like you know," Salazar yelled. "You never fuck before I do." He slammed the door closed behind him.

"What the fuck is this?" Carmen pushed Jas off her. "I ain't fuckin' them."

"Shit, I don't want you to."

"So, what is he talking about?" Carmen raged. "What are the rules?"

Jas rubbed the side of Carmen's face, climbing on top of her again. "We're a gift to them. Every so often, Presi sends his men up here to handle shit with Salazar. To show hospitality, Salazar lets 'em choose a girl for the night. The rule is we live out their fantasies. Condoms are recommended, but optional. They have us for the entire night. If they want longer, they pay."

"Get me the fuck outta here." Carmen pushed her onto the side of the bed. "I ain't fuckin' none of 'em." She balled up her fist. She wanted to text Lownes, but it was pointless. He was miles away in New York. It was on her to figure a way out.

Jas explained further. "They may not choose you. Or they may ask to watch. These men can be on some freak shit sometimes. Let's hope it's the latter. I know you wanna taste me."

I wanna punch you in your fuckin' face. Those words didn't leave Carmen's mouth. "If I have to fuck one of 'em, you're eatin' my pussy first."

Jas chuckled as she climbed off the bed. "Happily."

She grabbed Carmen's hand, about to lead her out the room, but Carmen remembered her breasts were out. She jerked her hand out her grasp and ran to her suitcase. She pulled out a pair of black pasties and covered her nipples while Jas waited in the hallway. When they ventured downstairs, a bunch of half-naked girls were headed inside the living room. Most of them appeared to be in their early twenties. They were all Hispanic or racially ambiguous-looking. With no one there who matched her complexion, her dark skin was guaranteed to stick out. She stepped in the doorway to see Salazar seated underneath the painting of *Carmen*. Two open suitcases and a money counter were on a coffee table. There were also two other men in the room. She wasn't shocked to see them, only shocked that one of them was her ex-husband.

"This is the address for the pick-up," Salazar was telling him.

"What pick-up?" Kane replied.

Don't look over here, don't look over here. Carmen was sweating bullets. *What is he doing here? He told me he was going to Miami. Like, what the fuck? I'm about to blow his cover. He's gonna see me and it's gonna be over. We're gonna die together.*

"Whatever you were told," Salazar mumbled. "Business is taken care of. Help yourself."

Kane looked at the women who had come in the room. He didn't know they were a part of the trip or that a pick-up was involved, but he wasn't turning down any pussy. He'd already made that mistake with Carmen. It was such a mistake he pulled over behind an abandoned building and rubbed one out. One hand was on his dick, the other holding his phone where he was watching her sex tape with Jay's best friend, Carlos. Carmen told him she was thinking of him when she slept with Carlos. That thought made the tape easy for him to jack off to.

In terms of what was in front of him, the ladies had the stereotypical video vixen look. Large breasts, small waists, with perfectly proportioned hips and asses. Their skin paired closer to Brick's than his own. They were a dream come true for a man who could never get a woman of that aesthetic. He bedded plenty of them, so their looks did nothing for his ego. It suited him to have an ebony queen so he could at least pretend he was smashin' Carmen or Monifah.

Salazar spoke behind him. "You can have the pick of the litter."

Kane watched as Brick walked towards the girls. He was stopping in front of each one like it was an inspection. *Shit, it is,* he thought. He looked at each woman in the line-up, before noticing the woman at the end. She was the only female whose skin looked like it was drenched in maple syrup. The sight of her made his dick stiffen. From where he stood, he examined her, starting at her feet. She was standing in nude Louboutin heels. *Carmen got twenty of those.* His gaze shifted to her thighs then to her hips, which was stamped with tiger stripes.

Carmen got those when she was carrying King.

He remembered their wedding night when he kissed them. He told himself he was going to give her more because she was going to carry all his kids. Months later, he learned he couldn't even give her one. His sperm count was too low for them to ever conceive naturally. *Damn, her titties are big. Those are fuckin' melons.* Her titties were bare, nothing covering them except an X-shaped pasty. *Carmen's breasts are that size.*

Everything about the woman took his mind to his ex. When he saw Brick nearing her, he moved. He may have been stuck with the Jay look-a-like, but they weren't friends. The last thing he wanted, is for him to take the one female in the room who favored his ex-wife.

He walked past Brick right as he was about to examine her. Kane then pushed him back as he recognized the woman. Everything about her reminded him of Carmen *because* she was Carmen. *No, she's not.* He blinked his eyes. *It's not possible. I left her in Brookstone. She's supposed to be watching Bella.* He blinked again. It was Carmen. The blonde highlights at the ends of her hair served as even more evidence. It matched his ex-wife's just like the shoes, the stretch marks, and her breasts.

Brick pushed his arm away, bringing him back to reality. "I'm trying to look at her."

"This one's mine," Kane said. His eyes were frozen on Carmen's, as hers was on his.

"We're a package," said the girl beside her.

Kane shot her a quick glance before looking back at Carmen. "Nah, I'm good with *her*."

"Kong knows what he wants, Jas." Salazar stood up as if he was going to intervene.

"Kong?" Carmen questioned.

Kane grabbed himself. "King Kong," he clarified. The move made Carmen smile. She turned towards the girl Salazar called Jas.

"I can handle this one. I promise."

Kane noticed the shocked expression on Jas' face. She looked at Carmen like she couldn't believe what she said. That's because she didn't know they used to be married. She also didn't know that in the morning, he was putting Carmen on a flight to Brookstone.

"Go upstairs," Kane told her. "Get that pussy wet for me. I'll be up in a minute."

"Use a room on the left," Jas whispered to her.

Carmen did as they said. Once she was gone, Kane went back to Salazar. He made sure the count was right before heading upstairs. Brick was in front of him, having picked two girls. He went in a room at the top of the hall while Kane walked further down until he found Carmen. A suitcase was at the foot of the bed, which he recognized as hers.

He locked the door behind him. The rest of the night was about to be hell. He looked at the ceiling, checking for cameras or smoke detectors. Not seeing any, he went to the closet, which was empty. He then pointed at Carmen. When she got to the doorway, he pulled her inside and held her against the wall.

"What the fuck are you doing here?" His volume was a whisper, but his tone was venom. "Is there something you forgot to tell me in Brookstone?"

"You didn't tell me you were coming to Vegas."

"I didn't know I was coming."

Carmen closed the closet door. "Well, now you know Dumati is linked to Salazar."

"I don't care about that right now. What I care about is how I'm gonna get you away from here." Kane grabbed his temples, his blood pressure rising. He paced the floor, trying to come up with a plan of how to get her out the house. He stopped pacing when an image of her in the line-up appeared in his mind. "Did you fuck him?" The him was Salazar.

"Hell no," Carmen spat.

"So, who did you fuck? You didn't get here without fuckin' somebody."

Carmen swallowed. She knew her tryst with Jas was something she could take to the grave. All she had to do was deny. For some reason, she didn't want to. "I had a moment with Jas."

Kane's eyes widened. "You did what?" It took a few seconds for her words to set in. When it did, he didn't take it as hard as the news of her being there. "You ate her out?" He asked the question with a smile.

"See, look at you, you ain't even mad anymore." She opened the closet door. She went back in the bedroom, Kane following her.

"Come on, Carm, you know that's one of my fantasies. I wanna watch."

"Karma," Carmen corrected. "Karma Levy, and to answer your question, no, I didn't."

Kane motioned for her to come closer to him. He didn't know much about Salazar, so he wanted to be careful as they talked. When she neared him, he pulled her into a hug, so his mouth could be at her ear. "Who helped you get here? I know you. You didn't do this shit on your own. Who was your Carlos?" The question got him punched in his stomach.

When she and Jay were first dating, she cheated on him with his best friend, Carlos. He also helped her steal Jay's diamonds and sell drugs behind his back. After learning of the deception, Jay killed Carlos and sent Carmen on her back to the hospital. Carlos' name was still a sore spot.

Still feeling the effects of the blow, Kane held onto her for support until the pain subsided. "Wrong choice of words. I'm sorry. Who helped you?"

"Your dick is hard."

"Ain't it supposed to be with you lookin' like that?" Kane lowered his arms and gripped her ass. He pushed her into him, so she could feel his print even more. "Now, you can really feel it."

"Let me suck it."

Kane buried his face in Carmen's neck. What she was asking, he wanted her to do, but they were on borrowed time. He had to get her out the house. The last thing he needed was the investigation compromised. "Tell me who helped you and I'll let ya."

Carmen broke his hold. "I thought you were gonna say no. I was trying to steer you away from your question."

"You're gonna be suckin' on him if you don't say something."

Kane pointed at the door. That realization did something to her because she sat on the bed.

"Torres Lownes," she revealed.

"Lownes?" Kane paced the floor again. "How did you link up with that son of a bitch?"

"Isn't this the son of a bitch who saved you when you planted a fake pink diamond?"

"He didn't do me a favor. I got dirt on his ass, too."

"Well, that's who helped me." Carmen moved further up the bed. She pulled the covers back and got underneath, but not before removing her jewelry and the pasties from her breasts.

With her nipples now visible, Kane placed his hand on his crotch. He was going to have to fuck something soon. "Who is he working for? The CIA, DEA, FBI?"

Carmen shrugged her shoulders. "He never told me. Sanders linked me with him."

Once again, Kane paced the floor. "I'm gonna break his neck."

"What's MXP?"

Kane stopped in his tracks as she unknowingly answered his question. He now knew what Lownes was up to. His former partner was smart. *He sent in someone he knew I would keep off the Triad's radar. He's following her every move. Once she gets close to Dumati, he's gonna pop up out of nowhere.*

"What's MXP?" she asked again.

"The agency Gully used to work for. They're bounty hunters."

Six

Carmen's eyelids fluttered open. She studied her surroundings, suspecting it to be around eight o'clock. She learned she was right when she grabbed her phone—7:48. Once she realized she was in bed alone, she sat up. She slept hard as Kane was able to make it out the room without waking her. While they kept their hands to themselves, they slept in a spoon. He hadn't gone far because he was now walking inside.

"Hey," she greeted. She pulled the covers up to her chest although he'd been staring at her bare breasts for most of the night. "Where were you?" He was fully dressed and in a different set of clothes than before. There was also a duffle bag in his hands.

"Talking to Salazar," he replied. "Good morning."

About to ask him what happened, he told her before she could.

"You're a thousand per day."

Carmen gave him a half-giggle. "That's bullshit. I'm not an escort."

"You became one when you came upstairs with me."

The remark made Carmen roll her eyes. "So, did you pay him?"

"With what?" he shot back. "I'm not here on my dime."

His attitude made her straighten her posture. "Okay, fine, you know I got the money. Did you tell him you would get it?"

"You act like you don't know what's going on."

"Well, say something. Shit," Carmen yelled.

The volume of her words made Kane drop his duffle bag. Just that quick, she forgot where they were. He moved closer to her, so his whispers would be audible. "You're priceless," was the first thing he said, "and I don't mean it like it sounds. It's not an option for you to stay in Vegas. You need to go home. It doesn't matter what he wants to charge." He paused before he gave her his next string of thoughts. "Let's say we give him the money. That covers you for today. It gives you enough time to get on a flight to New York. What do I do tomorrow? I can't make you magically reappear. We keep paying him until this thing is over?"

Carmen bit her lip. "This is bullshit."

"Lownes didn't prepare you for this, did he?"

Carmen pushed the covers off her. "I'll talk to Jas. Something's gotta give."

"There's other scenarios." Kane shared more of his thoughts. "Say we don't pay him, and you leave with me. I don't think he cares about you enough to try and find you. He ain't a sex trafficker. What am I gonna say to him if we cross paths again? Or what about this. How can I earn his trust if I'm not around him? We're only here to find Dumati. It'll be easier to do if I was in his house. Or even if I had someone in his house for me. That someone can't be you, though."

"Work your magic on Jas," Carmen suggested. "She dances at his club. Make her your inside person."

"That ain't gonna work. We're too far up shit's creek. Every road is a losing game."

A light bulb went off in Carmen's head. His words made her think about one of her favorite songs by Duncan Laurence. "Small town boy in a big arcade," she stated, reciting a lyric. "Who helped *you* get here? Why were you paying Salazar? You were paying him, right?"

Kane hadn't told her anything about Presi. He wasn't going to start either.

"Here's my plan," Carmen continued. "Make him an offer. Ten thousand in cash. He'll take it because I ain't shit to him. If it were Jas, he would want half a mill. That way I get out the house and don't have to fuck anyone. I'm also off his radar."

Carmen's words served as the perfect example of why men needed help meets. What she proposed was something Kane hadn't thought of on his own.

"Now we gotta get you on his radar," she continued. "You say you're King Kong, right?" Carmen straddled his lap. "King Kong isn't a small town boy. He's the arcade. Do what chu gotta do to get close to him. Make a name in his organization. Then, destroy the shit from the inside."

"I'll be getting in deep."

Carmen touched his lips. "Ain't that what you're here for?"

***

Getting ten thousand in cash was easy. Locating Salazar not so much. When Kane came downstairs, he expected to find him in the living room. The only person there was Leonardo Martí, one of Salazar's right-hands. He met him that morning when he first came down. He asked him about Salazar's whereabouts only for the man to coldly tell him, "He ain't here." Martí then followed it up with, "You shouldn't be either."

With Salazar nowhere to be found, Kane put Carmen in an Uber to get her away from the house. Meanwhile, he and Brick headed to Cohiba, Salazar's restaurant and cigar lounge, for the pick-up. They barely said two words to each other until Kane told him to put him on game. He still didn't know what they were picking up.

"Your guess is as good as mine," was Brick's response.

"How come you don't know?" Kane shot Brick a look. "You work for Presi."

"I work in Kingston, not Vegas."

Kane shot him another look before putting his eyes on the road. He was driving his new rental, a black Yukon Denali. "You gotta tell me something. Like, who are you? I know your mama didn't name you Brick. You ain't got an accent. You ain't Jamaican. How you link up with Presi?"

"Shit, you ain't Jamaican either," Brick shot back.

"Touché." Kane let the whole thing go. He was walking into the situation blind, but it wouldn't be a first.

Upon arriving at Cohiba, he put two pistols in his waistband. Salazar gave them an address but left out any information about a contact. If Kane knew Brick wasn't going to be any help, he would've asked Salazar for one. God was on his side because he ended up not needing it. The second they were inside, a man came up to them, telling them to park around back.

"Look for the Sysco truck," the man told them.

The quick directive told Kane that Salazar's men knew who they were. He wished he could say the same when it came to the boxes on the truck. There were too many in the semi-trailer for them to know which ones to take. The delivery driver wasn't any help, saying he was only there to drop off food.

"You gotta give me something," Kane said, staring at Brick. "Call Presi. You can't tell me you don't know anything."

"My job is to secure his estate, not cook."

"The only thing you're securing is your mouth." Kane reached inside his pocket, grabbing a knife. "I guess I gotta do this the hard way." He grabbed one box, cut it down the slit, and opened it. *Beef.* He pushed it aside. He went to the next one, coming up empty. When he grabbed the third, he noticed he was working alone. "Get a knife," Kane ordered. "Why are you standing here watching me work?"

Brick sucked his teeth. Despite his annoyance, he did as Kane said. While he was gone, Kane continued going through the boxes. In about twelve minutes, he opened fifteen boxes of nothing but meat, dairy products, and seafood. He didn't know what was keeping Brick, and he wasn't going inside to find out. He grabbed another box and sliced it down the middle. When he opened the flaps, bricks of cocaine were inside. "Checkmate." He held the box up, this time noticing the colored stripes on the side were different than the previous boxes.

"Got it," he whispered. He moved much quicker, now knowing what to look for. In the end, eight boxes were loaded in the Yukon. Brick hadn't returned. "The guy who was with me," he asked the delivery driver. "Did you see him when you went inside?"

"He's at the bar," the driver replied.

"This muthafucka," Kane griped. Brick was burying himself in a hole. "Fuck him." He stepped away from the truck ready to wash his hands of him. *If I had a number for Presi, I'd tell him about his ass. Shit, I'd ask him if I can gut him.* He glanced at the back door of the restaurant to see the driver heading inside with more boxes. With no eyes on him, he peered again at the truck. That was when he noticed a box that was different than the others. Noticeably smaller, it was tucked in between the larger food boxes. His interest peaked.

He climbed inside the truck and grabbed it. A piece of white typing paper was taped on one side of the box. In permanent marker, someone had written three different sets of numbers. For the sake of time, he didn't open it. Instead, he shifted the guns in his waistband to make room for it. He climbed out the truck, his arms carefully positioned to hide the box's imprint on his waist. Without any eyes on him, he got behind the wheel of the Yukon. He sped off, leaving behind everything and anyone that didn't matter.

***

Carmen wiped her face again feeling another tear. She was back in her room at Caesars Palace, now able to sort out everything she'd done. All the progress she'd made, working on herself, trying to be a better person, had flown out the window. At her age, she should've been mentoring girls like Jas, not playing around in their panties.

Another tear fell, sending her to the floor on her knees. She repented and asked God for forgiveness. After concluding the prayer, she prayed again. Prior to the crying spell, she called Rakim and Nyla. When they didn't answer their phone, she called Fiona. "They got their phone, I gave it to 'em," her maid said. Carmen heard her walking through the house. "Got dang it, Carm, it's dead. They were playing games on it and didn't put it on the charger. Let me get 'em."

Carmen waited for them to come to the phone. When they did, the joy she was missing returned. "Mommy, Mommy, Mommy." Their voices sounded like angels in heaven.

"We went and saw Daddy today," Nyla screamed. "He moved his hand."

"He didn't move his hand," Rakim argued. "You moved his hand."

"No, he moved his hand," Nyla screamed. "Then, I moved his hand."

Carmen broke down crying right there on the phone. She didn't know how long the kids were listening to her tears, but she heard Fiona when she took the phone away. Her maid confirmed Nyla's story, the guilt forcing Carmen to hang up the phone. It ate at her spirit, doubling, when Kane called her. Not wanting him to know she was upset, she put on her best act when she answered. "You're lucky," she greeted. "This phone was off. I turned it on because I forgot to put the kids' number in my burner."

"Then I am lucky," he said with a chuckle. "Where are you?"

"I have a room at Caesars Palace."

"That sounds good. Can I stay with you?"

That's what she didn't need. She may have repented for her sins, but her flesh was still weak. She chose not to answer the question. "What happened with the pick-up?"

"I don't wanna talk about that on the phone. Can I stay with you?"

"I'm confused," Carmen shared. "Why do you need to stay with me if I'm going back to Brookstone?" She posed the question despite having zero intention of leaving Vegas.

"You're going back, but not tonight. I need you for something."

Those words told Carmen one thing. He got another lead. "You can stay with me," she said, giving in. "I'm texting you my room number. It's in the Augustus Tower."

"I'm on my way."

She didn't know where he was coming from, but he arrived at her hotel room in less than twenty minutes. He came in the room with not only his duffle bag, but also a set of luggage. "Make yourself at home," she joked. She closed the door behind him before laying across the bed. He set his luggage on top of the sofa. He then unzipped his duffle bag, pulling out a box. "What's that?"

"We're about to see in a minute."

He set it on the café table in the living area. Instead of opening it, he joined her on the bed. "I picked that up along with some of Salazar's finest coke."

"That ain't a surprise." Carmen saw confusion on his face. "Wait, that is a surprise?"

He dropped his head in his hands. It took some time for him to get it out, but he came clean. He told her about Presi, their history, and what happened in Jamaica. He gave her the entire story from start to finish. "Now you see why I have a problem."

"You," Carmen began, pronouncing each of her words, "have bricks of cocaine parked in a Yukon at Caesars Palace. You don't even know why you have it. Presi didn't tell you to pick it up. He said deliver some money. Salazar told you to pick something up, but he didn't tell you what it was. You assumed it was drugs because Presi and Salazar are drug dealers."

"What else could it have been?" Kane countered. "Brick didn't know. He works for Presi."

"I was getting to that," Carmen retorted. "You stranded the one person who should've been able to help you. Look, I don't know anything about Brick. If you ask me, your best bet is finding him. It shouldn't be hard. There ain't a lot of men walking around here lookin' like Jay."

"Of course, you would want that."

Kane got up from the bed. He could feel Carmen's eyes on him.

"Oh," Carmen bellowed. "That's why you don't like him."

"Let's change the subject." Kane grabbed the box on the café table, pulling it closer to him. He stared at the numbers, trying to decipher the meaning:

47462357252927
562737833929
5278342789135

He took out his knife to loosen the tape around the handmade mailing label. Once he peeled it off, he read the address printed on the box. It was for one of Sysco's operating sites: Sysco Las Vegas, 6201 Centennial Parkway, Las Vegas NV, 89115. Whatever was in the box was either sent there first *or* originated there. He looked at the numbers again, studying them. Something told him it was a code, but he didn't have the energy to figure it out. He would need a hot meal, a good fuck, and a proper night's sleep to crack it. What he could handle was opening the box. He lifted the lid.

"Took you long enough."

He turned to see Carmen looking over his shoulder. "You better pray it ain't a bomb," he muttered. He pulled the lid all the way back to reveal a small velvet bag. The sight of it made Carmen gasp. Despite being caught off guard, it didn't stop her from pulling the box towards her.

Carmen untied the bag's strings. It was so weightless in her hands, she questioned if anything was in it. She squeezed it to get an idea. There was something there, but it felt like pomegranate seeds. Fed up with the suspense, she turned the bag over. When three red diamonds fell out, none of them larger than half a carat, she dropped the bag.

"I wasn't supposed to take that," Kane whispered.

You don't even know, Carmen thought. Red diamonds were a gem she'd never seen. Jay didn't even own one. The red stones sold in Iceland were all cubic zirconia. In fact, she was certain most of the world's population had never seen a red diamond. There were reports that only about twenty to thirty existed. Three of that possible thirty were in a box in her hotel room. "You have bricks of cocaine in a Yukon," Carmen repeated. "You now have almost two million dollars' worth of red diamonds in my hotel room." She stopped talking. Kane wasn't meeting her gaze. She stared him down until he did. "We are fucked."

SEVEN

The findings of the day had them both shook. Shook to the point they didn't leave the room for lunch or dinner. Carmen ordered room service, which she did again that morning for breakfast. Kane was finishing in the shower, having woken up before her.

The other day he mentioned there was something he wanted her to do. He said it was the reason he hadn't sent her back to Brookstone. Despite time being on their side, he never told her what it was. "Good morning," she greeted once he walked out the bathroom. "What's on the agenda?"

Kane replied in-kind, standing in front of her in one of the hotel's towels. "I gotta pick up my car from the Triad office. I need you to come with me, so you can drive the Yukon back to Enterprise."

Now confused, Carmen narrowed her eyes. "I don't mind doing it, but you don't need me for that. Not with the way you were going on and on about me being here. That doesn't sound like a reason for me to stay. One of the agents here can drive the car for you."

"They can. That's not what I want, though."

His response silenced her even more when he ditched the towel. *Oh, I see,* Carmen grabbed the remote from one of the bedside dressers. She turned the television on, hoping it would distract her from the temptation.

"You do know what today is."

Carmen didn't look his way, browsing through the channels until she found the local news. "It's not our anniversary. It's not our second anniversary. It's not your birthday. It's not my birthday. It's not even one of the kids' birthdays." She chuckled.

"Carm, it's Valentine's Day."

She looked at him right as he covered his manhood with a pair of boxer shorts.

"I didn't want to be alone," he added. "Can I celebrate with you?"

"Oh, so, now you wanna fuck?"

"I said celebrate, not fuck." Kane chuckled. "Damn, can I take you to dinner?"

"So, you feed me and then you wanna fuck?"

"I didn't say all that," he said with a laugh. "Is that what you want to happen?"

Carmen shrugged her shoulders. What she wanted and needed was two different things. What she did know was that she was fighting an internal battle within herself. The first time they messed around, Kane was the one begging for sex. Now, there were moments where he acted like he didn't want it. His words and actions left her feeling rejected, which she didn't like.

I want to be the one to turn him down. Not the other way around.

"Vegas police are searching for a killer after a delivery driver was found shot and stabbed outside the Sysco semi-trailer he was driving. The victim has been identified as thirty-eight year-old Ramirez Thomas. His body was found near Interstate 15."

The remote dropped from Carmen's hand. She glared at Kane whose eyes were now glued to the TV. She didn't even have to ask him. His face said it all. She turned off the television. "We're gonna pick up your car," she began. "Then, you're gonna give Salazar back his drugs."

Kane didn't like that idea. "I'm dead when I hit his gate. You heard what he did to him."

"Which is why you're gonna tell him it was a mistake. It's his fault he didn't tell you what to pick up. Ramirez's blood is on his hands and Presi's, not yours. Go to his house. Tell him it was a mistake and give him his shit back."

"That's fuckin' ludicrous, Carm."

Carmen stood up. "You don't get it," she said through gritted teeth. "The murders are starting. Ramirez is number one. Brick may be number two if he isn't already. Go to Salazar and apologize. Ask him again what you were supposed to pick up."

Kane dismissed the idea. "I'll turn it into the Triad. We'll raid his house, and we'll force him to give us Dumati for a lesser charge."

"Come on, Kane, I know what you Boy Scouts do. You do that, everyone in that house is getting arrested including Jas."

"I'm sorry I can't protect your girlfriend."

Carmen picked up the remote and threw it at him. He caught it, which is what she wanted. She threw it as a warning. "Play the game my way."

"Say I do," he replied, tossing the remote on the bed. "What are we gonna do about that?" He pointed at the box on the café table, which held the red diamonds.

"Oh, he ain't gettin' that. You tell him you took those diamonds, you're dead. Those diamonds ain't goin' anywhere. The stones are ours. It's gonna take care of our kids, our grandkids, our great grand-kids, our great-great grand-kids."

Kane scratched his chin as a new realization came to mind. "Dumati is still alive." He pointed again at the box. "Those diamonds came from him. You ain't gotta admit it, but I know Jay was picking up his diamonds at Flame. Dumati is sending diamonds to Salazar through Sysco. He shipped them there from Africa, Ramirez picked 'em up, so he could transport 'em to Cohiba."

"That's the best thing you've said all morning. Aside from wanting to take me to dinner."

Kane headed towards the bed about to kiss her, but his plan was interrupted by a knock at the door. "Get dressed," he said, hearing a woman yell room service. "It's about to be a day."

***

Yea, though I walk through the valley of the shadow of death, I will fear no evil: for thou art with me; Thy rod and thy staff they comfort me.

For the fiftieth time that morning, Kane recited Psalms 23. He recited it again as he pressed the call button outside Salazar's estate. A voice answered, which he recognized as Martí's. "Kong to see Salazar." He waited for a response. It never came, but after ten seconds or so, the front gate opened. When it did, he drove on the property. Martí met him in the driveway, both his hands empty. The man gave him an odd look when he stepped out the car, but he figured it was because he was now in an Escalade. The change in vehicles had Martí suspicious.

"Follow me," Martí ordered. "Although you know your way around."

If the situation weren't dangerous, Kane would've smiled. His life was on the line, so he kept a straight face. He followed Martí inside to find Salazar seated in the living room. The man looked stressed, which wasn't a good sign. "Good morning," Kane said to him, approaching the couch.

"Just say morning," Salazar ordered. "I'll decide if it's good."

Kane looked at Martí who was walking out the room. He then looked back at Salazar. "When we went for the pick-up yesterday, they sent us to a truck. I took some boxes, but I don't know if that's what I was supposed to get. If it wasn't, I have 'em here for ya. I apologize."

"Damn," Salazar said. "This is the first time I was robbed and got an apology."

"I'm sorry. I assumed the pick-up was the boxes because of my history with Presi."

Salazar picked up a mug from the coffee table. He took a few long sips of his coffee. "You said everything is there?" Kane nodded his head. "There were eight boxes, right?" Kane nodded again. "You're a blessed man, Kong. I would've shot you from my balcony if you didn't work for Presi. He saved your life."

"I'm sorry," Kane said again, not wanting Salazar to change his mind. "I can pull the boxes in for ya. I got 'em right in my car. Nothing has been touched."

Salazar shook his head. "I don't want it. You took it. You sell it. Bring me my money."

That was never Kane's plan. He didn't have a problem selling the drugs, he had a problem with the amount of drugs he had to sell. It would take months for him to sell all the bricks. He didn't have that kind of time to stay undercover. He wanted to get back home to Bella as soon as he could. Nevertheless, the deal was better than a bullet in his head. "Consider it sold," was his reply.

"If I don't get my money, you're dead. No second chances." Salazar reached inside his pocket. He pulled out a business card, which he handed over. "That's the address for the pick-up."

Kane read the card, seeing an address for La Gran Carnicería, a local butchery in Vegas. "So, there aren't any more mistakes, can you tell me what I'm picking up?"

Salazar took another sip of his drink. "What did Presi tell you to do?"

"He sent me here to deliver money to you."

"That task you completed." Salazar stood on his feet. "How's Karma? You would've been dead if I'd fucked her. Black women are the mothers of civilization."

Kane stuffed the card in his pocket. "Then you understand why I had to have her."

Salazar's lips curled into a smile. "She made a big impression on you. She also made one on Jas. You should let her stop by. You know, for some girl time."

Kane didn't respond to that offer. Carmen wasn't doing anything with Jas unless he could participate, too. "This pick-up," he said, changing the subject. "What am I looking for?"

"Figure out what Presi told you to do. Once you do it. Go to the address."

***

Carmen took a step away from the mirror, admiring her body in her dress. A chocolate brown, off the shoulder number, the bodycon dress not only matched her skin tone, it clung to it. She wore it on purpose, hoping Kane liked it enough to not mention anything about her going back to Brookstone. They may have been in a stressful situation, but peace came in knowing they had each other. *Speaking of Kane,* she thought. His number was now displayed on her burner phone. She answered, anxious to know what happened with Salazar. "Talk to me."

"I'm near the hotel. Go ahead and get ready for dinner."

"Oh, I'm ready," she said with a giggle. "You'll see when you get here."

Although she couldn't see him, she knew he was smiling. "Alright," he told her. "We'll see." The second he hung up, she called her kids. She didn't get them, which led her to call Fiona. Her maid answered on the first ring only to tell her the kids were at the hospital with Silvas.

"They have their phone, but service is wonky over there sometimes."

Carmen could agree it was. "I'll call 'em back and leave a message. Has Jay woken up?"

"No, he hasn't," Fiona mumbled. "We thought he was going to because of what happened yesterday. That's why the kids have been up there."

"If he does, call me. I don't care what time it is."

"You know I will."

Carmen whispered goodbye before calling her kids again. She left them a message, letting them know she was thinking of them, and she loved them. When she hung up from the call, Kane was coming in the room. Although she was still in the bathroom, he didn't hesitate to tell her about his conversation with Salazar.

"I'm gonna be here for a good three or four months."

Kane shook his head over the matter. Hearing Carmen's footsteps, he looked towards the bathroom. She was standing in the doorway wearing a dress that looked painted on. There he was, trying to hold back from doing her, only to be seconds away from succumbing. "Is that for me?"

"We can talk about it after dinner." Carmen sat on the bed. "Right now, we need to deal with this coke. We need to get it out your car."

"I already got a plan. In the morning, I'm going to the Triad office. I'ma have them rent me an apart—" He stopped talking when he saw Carmen drop her head. "You got a better idea?"

"You know Floyd has been living here for years. He can recommend a realtor. Let me buy a house. The process shouldn't be long. I don't need a lender."

"I can't let you do that."

"You can't or you won't?" Carmen needed him to clarify.

Kane didn't have to think twice. "I won't. After tonight, you're going back home."

So, the dress didn't work. Carmen pretended to ignore him. She picked up her purse and retrieved her cell. She then called Floyd. Once named Fighter of the Decade, the boxer was not only known for his skills in the ring, but also for his playboy lifestyle and lavish mansions. She didn't expect to get him on the first try since he was a busy man, but when he answered, it was obviously a part of God's plan. "It's been a while," she told him after he said hello.

"Don't tell me you're in Vegas," he said with a laugh.

"I am," she said, glancing at Kane. He didn't look happy, but he also wasn't doing anything to stop the call. "I need some help." She summed up what she needed and how fast.

"I may have somebody for ya. Come by Girl Collection tonight."

"Done," Carmen replied. After a few more exchanges, she was off the phone.

"You thought that was the right thing to do?" Kane didn't even care to hear her response. She was right about a lot of things when it came to the case, but he still wanted full control.

"A house provides privacy an apartment can't. With a house, you can put the coke in the basement. You put it in an apartment, you're gonna be cutting coke with the maintenance man looking over your shoulder. Think like Kong, not Kane."

"You don't want me to think like Kong."

"Ugh, right now, I do." She watched as he sorted through the clothes in his suitcase. When he pulled out a camel-colored long-sleeve shirt and a pair of brown slacks, she smiled. They hadn't worn matching outfits in a long time. About to say something to him about it, the ringing from her phone stopped her. "You work quick," was the first thing she said to Floyd.

"I'm dealing with you," he joked. Floyd shared he had a business partner who was moving out the country. He put his home up for sale but was struggling to find a buyer. "The asking price is twelve million. Carm, I promise you. The house is legit. Now, it ain't got nothing on my shit, but it's up there," he said with a chuckle. "He's a bachelor, so it looks like a party house. It's fully furnished, which is why he's asking for twelve. He's already moved out. It has five bedrooms, nine bathrooms, multiple garages. I told him who you were. While he would prefer to have a promise contract or a proof of funds letter, we know you can't get that tonight. I'm gonna front you some cash, like a little deposit, on good faith. You can pay me back tomorrow once the banks open."

"Can I have the address," was the next thing out Carmen's mouth. Once he gave it to her, she used her burner phone to locate pictures of the home. When she saw it, she knew it was perfect. Regardless of what Kane said, the house was hers. "First thing in the morning, I'll get your money."

"Come by the club as planned. He'll be there. He'll give you what you need."

After thanking him twelve times over, Carmen hung up the phone. She was now in the bedroom alone as Kane was in the shower. When he emerged, she told him five words.

"Time to be an arcade."

EIGHT

If there was a third party in the car, they would've suspected there was tension. Neither one of them was speaking while Carmen's body was turned towards the window. Like her, Kane was lost in his thoughts. He was driving to Sugar Factory, the restaurant where he and Carmen had dinner reservations. Prior to that, they had been outside the house Carmen was purchasing. She wanted him to see it, so when they went to Girl Collection that night, there wouldn't be any issues. Little did she know, his entire mindset had changed. She mentioned she wanted him to think like Kong and that was what he was going to do.

The moment he saw the house, he knew it was meant for him. It was sexy, stylish, and designed specifically for a man with money and power. "You like?" Carmen asked, rubbing his back. He didn't tell her he did. He showed her. He placed a soft kiss on her lips. He then walked to the car, making that the last moment they spoke. That was all about to change, though.

"When you talk to Floyd," he began, seeing the turn come up for the Fashion Show mall, "ask him about getting in on our operation."

"Huh? What are you talking about?"

"We gotta sell that shit somewhere," Kane told her. "I ain't workin' no corners. We need to run the coke through his club. If shit gets hot, I'll let the Triad know he was helping me. When we take down Dumati, they'll give him a medal."

Carmen disagreed. "We should run it through Salazar's clubs, not his."

"We're gonna do that, too. I just didn't say it. Talk to Jas. No fuckin,' though."

Carmen raised her brow at his tone. In fact, she looked to make sure it was really him. He wasn't sounding like himself. He felt her eyes on him, returning the glare.

"Happy Valentine's Day," he whispered.

The words shifted her mood. "Happy Valentine's Day." She ran her fingers along his chinstrap beard. "You said we should run it through Floyd's club."

"Your job tonight is to make sure that happens."

"You said we," she repeated. This time he caught on.

"Can I kick you out your own house?"

Carmen knew he was driving, but she didn't care. She grabbed his face and pulled it towards hers. She kissed his cheek repeatedly, catching his lips a couple of times in the process. "I knew you were gonna let me stay."

"You forced my hand, but it is what it is." He turned into the mall's parking lot. "No more business talk, aight?" Carmen agreed. They stuck to the plan, enjoying each other's company without talks of Salazar, drugs, or the Triad. When dessert hit the table, they weren't talking at all. They were stuffing their mouths with spoonfuls of the restaurant's Strawberry Cheesecake Overload.

"I can't keep eating like this," Carmen moaned. "I won't be able to wear my clothes."

"You won't have to," Kane replied. "You'll have a kitchen to cook in." They met eyes, both wearing a grin, until Carmen's turned upside down.

"Oh, shit," she mumbled.

"What's wrong?" He turned to see Brick near the bar with a few shopping bags. When he charged at him, Kane stood from his seat, catching Brick at his waist. He tackled him to the floor, keeping the upper hand as Brick squirmed underneath him.

"Stop, stop, I'm calling the cops," someone screamed from afar.

Kane overlooked the voice. What Brick didn't know was that he was a man with pent up aggression. He'd buried his wife only weeks ago, had a newborn in the NICU, and was in love with his ex-wife who was married to a person he hated. The stress of it all made him want to be tested. He wanted someone to say something to him. In this case, that someone was Brick. Presi's right-hand gave Kane what he wanted. It was easy to fight him because every time he punched him, he thought he was punching Jay. About to strike him again, heavy arms separated them.

"You son of a bitch," Brick yelled.

A strong, "fuck you," came out the back of Kane's throat. "You ain't worth shit."

"We're leaving," he heard Carmen say. She was handing their waitress her debit card. That was all Kane needed to get to his feet. She had been the ATM for most of their stay. The last thing he was going to do was let her pay for dinner.

"I got it," he told the waitress. "Give her the card back."

"You son of a bitch," Brick repeated.

"Go outside and wipe your face," Kane ordered, pulling out his wallet. "Standin' up here bleedin' every got damn where." He handed the waitress his card. She was quick, running with it behind the bar. "Are you okay?" he asked Carmen.

"Oh, I'm peachy," she replied. "Are you okay? You just whooped ass."

He knew it wasn't anything to smile about, but he did. That was until he was outside the restaurant with Brick still in his face.

"That was some bullshit," Brick growled. He spat out blood.

"What's bullshit is you sittin' your ass at a bar instead of gettin' Presi on the line."

"Presi didn't give me no fuckin' job," Brick shot back. "He told me to come with you."

"That's the job, muthafucka," Kane shouted. "We're in this shit together."

Carmen slid in between them. "All right, we gotta get somewhere with this." She touched Kane's chest hoping the affection would calm him. "Look, I know y'all hate each other, but right now, we need every man we can get. Can we table this for tonight and regroup sometime tomorrow?"

"Fuck his ass," Kane yelled.

When he spit in Brick's direction, Carmen knew to dead the issue. Her ex wasn't in any mood to compromise. He walked off from them, heading to the car. Left to deal with Brick alone, she stared at him, his face looking like he came out an MMA fight. "Do you have a place to stay?"

"When did you hoes start talkin'? Matter of fact, what is he doin' witchu?"

The question made Carmen blink her eyes. Brick was right. *What was Kong doing with her? In his world, she wasn't anything, but a one-night stand.*

"It doesn't even matter, hoe." Brick snatched up his shopping bags. When he headed back in the restaurant, Carmen walked away although she wanted to beat his ass, too.

"Well, there goes our pleasant evening," she said to Kane once she was in the Escalade.

"We ain't gonna let him ruin our night. Where did he go?"

Carmen summed up her brief conversation with Brick. Kane suggested they forget about him. Carmen didn't think it was an option. Brick could've easily flown back to Jamaica, but he stayed in Vegas for a reason. She wanted to find out why.

"If it ain't Mrs. Santiago," Floyd greeted.

They were now standing in the VIP Black section of Girl Collection. Two half-naked dancers surrounded Floyd. "Money Mayweather," Carmen greeted. He stood up to give her a hug. After the embrace, she noticed the puzzled look on his face. He pointed at Kane. "We're out here on business," she explained.

"Jay wouldn't be cool with that."

Carmen gave him a quick update. "What he doesn't know won't hurt him. He's still in a coma. Thank you for asking."

"My apologies. I didn't know. My prayers are with y'all." Floyd signaled to one of the dancers. "Take care of him." He then looked at Kane. "Dances and drinks, on me."

"Whoa, whoa." Carmen stepped in between the two. "Don't disrespect me like that."

Floyd became even more confused. "Y'all back together or something? Let the man get a dance. Is he a part of *our* business?"

The answer to the question was yes, but Carmen was certain Kane wanted her to handle Floyd on her own. While she met Floyd during their marriage, the two never hit it off. Jay and Floyd, on the other hand, did. They were both businessmen, which gave them lots in common. "It's cool," she finally said. She peered at Kane, telling him with her eyes to be on his best behavior. After he left, Floyd excused the other stripper.

"Where's your partner?" she asked, aware there was supposed to be a third party.

"He said something came up. He sent me the info you need, though. I got the gate codes, and he had an assistant drop off the keys." Floyd reached in his pocket, handing the items to her. "Keep it real with me, though. What cha here for? You ain't been on this side of the country in years. You got me curious. I mean, you did walk up in here with him."

Carmen hadn't prepped herself on what she was going to say. Brick messed all that up. Somehow, the words came to her, anyway. At first, Floyd wasn't feeling the idea of being a part of anything with the Triad. He quickly reminded her it was ITIA who took down her husband. She then reiterated to him that the organization was also working on taking down the man who shot him. That got Floyd to consider the offer. After agreeing to a few financial terms, and a promise to make a couple club appearances, they were squared away.

Carmen stood from her seat. "How many private rooms I gotta knock on to find him?" Kane hadn't returned, which meant he was still with the stripper or at the bar.

Floyd smiled. "He can be in one of nine."

Carmen rolled her eyes. "You gonna make me smack a bitch. I'll call you in the morning." She left the area, hearing Floyd laughing behind her. She headed towards the VIP lounge, cracking open door after door to see if Kane was inside. She opened about six of them, almost walking in on several patrons getting more than dances. When she cracked open the seventh door, it was no different. A man had a stripper bent over, taking her from the back. It took only a second for her to recognize Kane. "You fuckin' asshole." She slammed the door against the wall.

He yelled something at her, but she was already running from the room. *I hate him, I fuckin' hate him.* She ran through the club, trying to get as far away as possible. *I wasn't even gone twenty minutes. He was fuckin' that bitch raw.* She ran outside the club, tears and snot flying down her face. *I'ma kill him, I'ma kill him.* She grabbed her head, still seeing the image of him pounding the girl. *You fuckin' asshole. You dirty ass motherfucker.*

"Carm, come here."

"Fuck you." Carmen swung hard, connecting with the side of Kane's head. He took the punch like a champ. "Get away from me." He grabbed her, leading her to swing again. That punch caused him to stumble. It also caught the eye of one of the club's bouncers. He came over to mediate, but they were already separating from one another.

"You know that didn't mean shit to me," Kane argued.

"Fuck you," she screamed again.

"Man, I got this," Kane said, noticing the bouncer. "We're fine."

"Nah, I'm gonna stick around, brotha." The bouncer looked at Carmen. "She ain't fine."

Carmen took off heels, now unable to stand in her shoes. She walked to the car although it was the last place she wanted to be. There she was, trying to help them move forward so they could get back home, and he showed her the upmost disrespect.

"You know that didn't mean shit." Kane grabbed her from behind, holding her to his chest. "It was a fix. I just needed a little fix." His words didn't make anything better. For two nights in a row, they slept beside each other. At any time, he could've rolled over, and she would've taken care of him. "She didn't mean anything." He planted kisses on her shoulder blades. "You know that."

His apologies only made her cry harder. The act hit a sore spot, reminding her of the time he cheated on her with Tricia. They were in the middle of their first divorce but made the agreement to work on their marriage. She was doing her part, only to discover Kane wasn't. His infidelity sent her back in Jay's arms, which was how she ended up pregnant with Nyla.

Kane pulled away from her, unlocking the Escalade's doors. She got inside, her countenance the same, her tears fleeting. The mood was only temporary. Halfway to the house, on S. Rainbow Blvd., she lost it. She didn't know how many times she punched him, but it was enough to make him grab her by the throat. His free hand struggled to keep the car from oncoming traffic.

"Are you tryin' to kill us?" He pulled in the parking lot of a shopping center.

All Carmen could do was cry. When her tears dried, he pulled into the street. Once they made it to the house, she left him in the driveway. Her first time being inside, she couldn't even enjoy the home's beauty. Too distraught to look around, she headed up the steps. On the second floor, she opened each door until she found the master bedroom. The room was partially lit a royal blue, the tint coming from the swimming pool down below. In the dark, she crept towards the bed, dropping her heels on the floor. Without any more energy to give, she passed out.

When she did wake, she laid there for a few minutes staring at the blue light pouring in the room. A different type of ambience, the light gave the room a calming vibe. She stared at it, knowing it would disappear with the waking sun. Then, it stared at her as she struggled to keep her eyes open. Before she could head into another slumber, she turned over in bed. Her eyes were open long enough to see Kane lying shirtless beside her. Tears streamed down his face. It was pleasant for her to see. She wanted him to hurt. She wanted him to feel every emotion of guilt. He deserved to.

His tears were short-lived, though. He sat up, his face now dry, giving her the impression he was about to leave. Instead, he moved his frame over hers. Curious as to what he was about to do, she remained still. His hands pushed the bottom of her dress towards her waist. He then dug his fingers through the strings of her panties, pulling off her underwear. He spread her legs apart, centering his head in between them.

His tongue gave her clit a slight graze. He did it several times, teasing her, before giving it a more forceful lick. That one made her body tense up. The second one he gave, more aggressive than the first, made her hands grab the sheets. He plunged deeper, spelling out her name with each lick.

She told him not to stop. She begged him to make her cream. She whispered her pussy was his. Her words only made him please her more. He placed two fingers inside her, the quick thrusts sending her into a fit of moans. His name echoed off the walls. Kane drove her into a pit of euphoric insanity. Her pussy throbbed from his goodness, forcing her to release inside his mouth. "I love you," she whispered. Still in bliss, she felt his head rest on her stomach.

He then repeated the words.

NINE

The Las Vegas heat woke Carmen up. She was in a pool of sweat, which told her the air conditioner wasn't on. Whether it had been the night before, she didn't know. She was too out of it to notice. Now, the first thing on her mind, she sat up. She stared at Kane's side of the bed to see a note was left in his place. *I have some business to take care of,* it read. *Call me when you wake up. I know I need to take you to the bank.* She read the note again before reading the last two sentences. *I love you. Please forgive me.* That part made her close her eyes. Despite being intimate with him, she wasn't over what he did. She only put a band-aid over it. Her plan for the day was to use some alone time to work on forgiveness. That was why she didn't call him.

After getting dressed, she spent the first part of her morning unpacking, exploring the house, and changing the gate codes, which she texted to Kane. She took an Uber to the bank to transfer Floyd his money and to acquire the paperwork she needed to purchase the house. From there, she took another Uber to a car dealership. With a letter from the bank confirming the amount in an account she shared with Jay, she wrote a check for a brand new black Mercedes Benz C-Class. Once the keys were in her hand, she called Floyd. He put her in contact with a realtor to represent her on the sale and the home's owner. About an hour later, she had appointments booked for an inspection and appraisal.

She moved to her next task, which was buying all the things the home needed. Pots, pans, cookware, dinnerware, everything needed to make a house a home. She then dropped the items off at the house before leaving again to go grocery shopping. Kane hadn't called to check in, which meant he knew they needed their space. King did call, able to reach her because her personal cell was still on from her call with Floyd. "Hey, firstborn," she joked.

"I'm surprised you remembered. Your grown kids don't get daily phone calls."

"I didn't call y'all every day when I was home," she said with a chuckle.

"This is different, Ma. You need to check-in."

Carmen told him she would do better.

"I just got off the phone with Dad," he said, speaking of Kane. He still referred to him as such while he affectionately called Jay, Pops. "He asked for something that didn't sit right with me. Why didn't you tell me he was out there with you?"

"That's another story," Carmen replied. "What did he ask for?"

"The crew we had out there when we were slangin'. We were just hitting the West Coast when Jay shut the cartel down. I only met one of those dudes. That's the only number I got."

Smart move, Kong, Carmen thought. "Give it to him. If anything goes down, he'll make sure they're protected. He knows what he's doing."

"That's all I needed to hear. I'll call him back." The line went silent for a few seconds. "Look, I know it's not my business—" Carmen interrupted him.

"Then don't ask," she told him.

"Are you sleeping with him?"

"Jayceon King Santiago, if you don't get off my phone."

"He started talking about how he hurt you and how he gotta make it right. He ain't talked like that since—"

"King, I love you. Goodbye." She hung up the phone. *Why did you do that?* she asked, thinking of Kane. *Yes, King is grown, but keep his ass out our business.* She cringed. The last thing she needed was her infidelity with Kane on King's radar.

Not wanting to think about it any longer, she continued shopping, racking up a three hundred dollar bill. She returned home to see Kane was there. "Hey," she said to him, placing bags of groceries on the kitchen's island. He responded to her the same. She expected him to ask why she didn't call, but he only told her he was going to help with the groceries. While he went outside, she headed upstairs with a few bags of personal items. She set them in the master bathroom and on her way out, she noticed a bouquet of white roses on a dresser. Certain the roses were for her, she went to check them out.

I'm still fixing all the cracks, was written on the note. It was a line from the Duncan Laurence song, "Arcade," she had been thinking about the past couple of days. Kane was trying to make up with her. His effort made her cut him some slack. She also did it because he hadn't done anything wrong. He was a widower, and she was married to someone else. He could sleep with whoever he wanted to. She didn't have a single hold on him. Matter of fact, she slept with someone, too. While it wasn't initially for pleasure, she still had done it.

"Do you like 'em?"

She hadn't even heard him come up the stairs. "I do." She gave Kane a smile. "I appreciate it." She opened her arms for a hug. He fell in her bosom, the embrace sending them into a kiss.

The moment intensified, leading Kane to pull away. "Let's save that for tonight. We start now, we won't get anything done."

"You got a point there. After what you did last night, I wasn't good for no one."

Her remark made him chuckle. "You've been eating your pineapples."

Carmen giggled before telling him she was heading downstairs. He followed her to the kitchen where they used the time to unpack the groceries and catch each other up. Although the kitchen was stocked with food, Carmen ordered takeout as they had a taste for sushi. After sharing a meal, she headed upstairs to shower and to turn into Karma. Kane told her to talk to Jas about selling the coke in Salazar's club. Her plan for the night was to make sure that happened.

This time, she chose a wine-colored mini dress that left little to the imagination. Another balconette style, there were cutouts at the bottom of the chest area that displayed her underboob. There were also large circular cutouts down the sides of the dress, which had been accentuated with rhinestones. She paired the dress with a diamond studded stiletto. After styling her hair and putting on a fresh set of makeup, she headed downstairs for Kane's approval.

He had taken off his shirt and was sitting on the couch in a black wifebeater and jeans. An old re-run of *Empire* played on the wall-sized television. "Do you think this will do the trick?"

He motioned for her to come near him. When she did, he pulled her into his lap. "It's working on me." He gave her a firm kiss.

"When I get back," she told him with a giggle. "I promise."

"Some people are supposed to be stopping by. You may see some fresh faces."

Carmen climbed off his lap, thinking back to her conversation with King. "Sounds good, thanks for the heads up." She gave him another kiss before heading out. The drive to La Zona Roja was longer than the first. This time, she knew what to expect. She also knew Jas would want an explanation for why she slept with Kong. She came up with one during the drive in the event she asked. Glad she had, the question was posed. It just wasn't the first or second thing out Jas' mouth. Carmen found her at the bar, talking to the same bartender from the night before. Like Jas did her, Carmen palmed her ass to get her attention. Once she had it, she headed to one of the club's VIP rooms.

Jas followed her inside, closing the door behind her. She was dressed in a red lace mini dress, which showed all her goods. "I only got twenty," Jas shared. "I have to get dressed for my dance." She didn't allow Carmen to respond. "You remember the guy that was with Kong? I think his name is Brick. He came by the house today. It didn't go so well."

"What happened?" Carmen sat on the couch, wondering if Jas was about to tell her he'd been murdered. It wasn't a good look if there were two people in Vegas wanting to end his life.

"They roughed him up. I don't know what it was about. I thought you knew."

Carmen shared what happened the night before. "I saw him at Sugar Factory. He and Kong got into it."

"Oh, the guy you left with. Salazar told me y'all are together."

"I was gonna talk about that."

Jas dismissed the topic. "You don't have to. If that's what you want, that's what you want."

"You don't mean that," Carmen told her. "I can tell from your tone you're not happy about it. Kong's a different person from what you saw that night. We didn't even sleep together. We talked. He understood I was uncomfortable. I explained to him what happened."

"Does he know what we did?"

Carmen nodded. "So, you don't know what's going on with Brick?" She switched the topic on purpose. Brick's behavior had her curious. Things with him weren't adding up.

"I know he's staying at the Luxor Hotel. I heard him tell Salazar."

Carmen got an idea. "I need to pay him a visit."

Jas joined her on the couch. She leaned in for a kiss, which led Carmen to put her index finger on her lips. "I can't."

"Because of Kong, right?"

"I know it's fucked up, but yes." Carmen's words made Jas move farther away from her. "I need a favor from you," she continued, not forgetting the reason behind her visit. "I don't know how much Salazar tells you, but Kong has a lot of weight to sell for him. Do you think it's possible for him to use the club?" Jas' eyes widened. "I don't know if that look is good or bad."

"Salazar doesn't run his drugs through the club. He says it's like shittin' where you eat."

"Well, in this case, he wouldn't be. Kong is."

"I know how it can be done," Jas admitted. "People bring drugs in the club all the time. Can I get a cut if I help you?"

"Of course, I gotta take care of my girl."

"Your girl?" Jas questioned.

"You know what I meant." Carmen grabbed her hands. "Is it a deal?"

"If Kong lets me have another night with you."

It was Carmen's eyes who widened this time. She even dropped her hands. Her eyes didn't stay that way for long as she remembered something Kane said. *You know that's one of my fantasies. I wanna watch.* "I think we can work that out. Do we have a deal?" She extended her hand to Jas. She shook it, which made Carmen's lips form into a smile. "Let me get your number. I'll text you a time when we all can meet." Carmen pulled the burner phone out her purse. After they exchanged numbers, she was back in her Benz, headed to Luxor. Her plan was to wait in the lobby to see if Brick showed.

It ended up taking an hour and a half before she saw him. He was coming off an elevator, and like Jas said, he'd been roughed up. A fresh scar was under his left eye. She hurried towards him, only for him to see her before she was close. She could tell he was willing to talk when he headed her way.

"Can we get a drink?" she asked him.

That was all she needed to say for them to end up at a table inside Aurora, a bar located in the lobby of the hotel. They both ordered drinks although he was the only one sipping. "Why didn't you go back to Jamaica?" was the first question she asked him.

"You're not like those other girls at Salazar's house," he said.

"Why would you say that? We've barely interacted."

Brick sipped his drink. "Cause you're the only piece of pussy askin' me about Jamaica. The bitches I fucked ain't even thinkin' 'bout me. Why are you? Why do I peak your interest?"

Carmen could admit the questions he was asking was legit. Her actions were suspicious. "Kong has a lot of weight to sell for Salazar. He needs all the men he can get. You're a stranger, but you're not a stranger. I want to help y'all build a bridge."

"You said he's sellin' weight for Salazar?"

"The boxes he took from the truck contained nothing but bricks," Carmen confirmed.

Those words intrigued him. "What's your name again?"

"Karma," she replied. She grabbed a napkin and wrote her number on it. She slid it to him. "If you're willing to help, I'll handle Kong." Brick told her he would think about it. "That's better than nothing." She slid her drink his way. "Cheers."

With those words, she left him in Aurora. She returned home to find fresh faces like Kane said in their living room. Most of the men appeared to be Hispanic, which is how she knew they were once a part of the Santiago cartel.

"Gustavo, Orestes, Jose, Felix." Kane pointed at each man. "Patheros, Chico, Julio, and Lomax. Fellas, you've heard of Carmen, but you're gonna call her Karma." The men waved at her. "They're gonna be in the basement. You know, cuttin' some stuff."

"Sounds like a long night," Carmen replied.

"I told 'em you were a good cook," Kane said. "Can you whip up some breakfast for 'em in the morning?"

Carmen was all for it. "That's the least I can do. How about some salmon bites, grits, and homemade biscuits?"

"Sounds good to me," Felix said.

Carmen wandered over to Kane and tapped his shoulder. "Can I talk to you for a minute?" He gave her a questionable look as if to ask was he in trouble. "Good news," she said to soothe his nerves. Those words got him up the steps. When he closed the door to their bedroom, she filled him in on her conversations with Jas and Brick. He agreed to Jas' proposal, but only if she agreed he could watch. Brick, however, was a different story.

"You thought it was a good idea to go to his hotel?"

"You have to figure this shit out with him," Carmen pressed. "You're gonna have to talk to Presi at some point." Kane still wasn't rocking with the idea of having Brick on his team. "Let me cook a nice dinner and you two can sit down and talk about what happened. I feel like he knows something. He's still here for a reason. You left him stranded, but he shouldn't have been as mad as he was. You don't owe him anything."

"I don't. I don't even know why Presi made me bring him. He's full of bitchassness."

Carmen giggled at his choice of words. "That's Kong talkin'," she whispered. "Check this out, Brick is even suspicious of me. He said the girls he slept with ain't even worried about him." She laughed again until a new thought entered her mind. She was hesitant to ask, but a part of her was curious. "If I hadn't been at Salazar's house, would you have slept with one of those girls?"

"You were in another room, and I slept with someone. Although, I didn't finish."

She bit her lip. "When you were in Jamaica before, did you cheat on me?"

"Please don't start this."

"You did," Carmen muttered.

"Why are you assuming I did?" Kane's voice was now raised.

"Because if you hadn't, you would've said no. How many women were there?"

"I'm going downstairs to check on the guys. Be naked when I come back."

Carmen stepped in between him and the door. "How many women were there?"

"Why do you wanna know? What is it gonna do? I didn't care about them bitches just like I didn't care about the bitch from last night. It was a nut."

The tears were coming fast down Carmen's face like the night before. "This whole time I thought I was the one who broke our covenant, but you did. You were wide open long before me."

"I fucked women whose name I didn't know. You fucked a guy you wanted to marry."

Kane tried to leave the room again. She blocked his path. "How many?" Carmen asked. She wasn't going to let up. She wanted to know. In fact, she wanted to know everything. "Tell me."

"So, you can be hurt again? It was eighteen years ago. I didn't get anybody pregnant. I didn't bring anything home. It meant nothing."

"How many?" Carmen asked again.

"Forty," he replied.

Carmen almost vomited on the floor. "You said you were only with four women. You said those were long-term relationships. I thought I was number five. I knew six and seven were Tricia and Monifah, but you've been with forty-seven," she shrieked. "What you did in Jamaica is like…"

"Some were at the same time."

Carmen slapped him. "You disrespectful motherfucker. You slept with forty bitches and then brought your dick home to me."

Kane raised his hand, but it went no further than that. "Let that be the last time you hit me. First," he said through gritted teeth. "I would never do that. I stayed with another agent, made sure I was clean then I came home to you."

"Oh, so you fucked 'em in a shorter amount of time?"

Kane gave her all his skeletons. He wanted this to be the last time he put anything on the table. "I also killed five men while I was there. Judge McCallum's blood is on my hands, too."

Carmen backed away from him. Judge McCallum was Brookstone's oldest living judge until his death. Kane was in his chambers when he passed, but she never thought he killed him. The news reported McCallum's cause of death was a heart attack. "I don't even know who you are."

"I'm the man you wanted me to be—Kong."

Carmen opened the door. "Get out."

"Back in the fuckin' doghouse again." Kane walked past her, yet he stopped once he hit the doorway. "I ain't got nuthin' else to hide. My shit is on the table. I was wildin', but I wasn't just out there wildin'. Get my drift? The job gave me something I never had." He faced her. "I didn't grow up being Jay Santiago. I didn't have the nice curly hair, the light skin, the colored eyes. He ain't gotta speak and he can get some pussy. In Jamaica, I saw what that life was like. I got caught up. I wasn't leaving home, though. I didn't care about them bitches."

Carmen wiped her face. "They gave you the ego boost I couldn't. You didn't need any of that for me. I loved you the way you were." A new tear fell. "What happened between you and Lownes? I mean, aside from the pink diamond." She felt there was more to the story.

"I fell in love with you."

Carmen listened as he told her about the conversations he had with Lownes. "Don't wife the bitch," Lownes told him. "She should be like the others, a fun time." Kane didn't follow his advice, leading Lownes to request a reassignment. He thought Kane was jeopardizing the case.

"You should've put your dirt on the table a long time ago. Mine was always there."

"Was it?" Kane asked. "Let me ask you a question." He scratched his chin. "Were you in love with me when we got married?"

Out of everything he could ask, Carmen never expected that. The question had never come up before. Since they were playing the Truth Game, she gave it to him. "No," she replied, "I wasn't. I knew I loved you. I knew you were a good person. I didn't realize I was in love with you until all I wanted in this world was to carry your child. That was months later."

"That's what I thought. I guess everything is now on the table. Is this a new slate for us?"

Carmen shrugged her shoulders. She didn't know what it was. She was numb. "Take care of your men. I'm going to bed." She turned away, stripping herself of her clothes. By the time she was naked, the door was closed, and he was downstairs. She escaped into the bathroom where another round of tears started. The shower was therapeutic as she was able to analyze everything Kane told her. She didn't know what it was like to walk in his shoes. Growing up, guys were attracted to her until she told them she was abstinent. Jay was her first big love. Any guy before him wasn't around long enough to make an imprint on her heart.

Carmen got inside the bed, this time thinking of Monifah. Right before she was murdered, Monifah told her she wasn't in love with Kane. She only married him to get back at her. The idea crossed Carmen's mind to tell him until she realized it wasn't her truth. It was Monifah's. The secret was meant to go to the grave. Kane was wearing enough pain, which she saw when his tears woke her up hours later. The night before, he was hurting, but he gave her a ticket to Pleasure Island. She now felt like she needed to give him one back.

She kissed his lips, but he didn't return the affection. She tried a second time. He put forth effort, but there wasn't any passion. She kissed him again. This one he returned. Moments later, she positioned herself over his manhood. She hadn't even gotten him hard before he stopped her.

"I want to see it."

His words made Carmen move to the opposite side of the bed. She knew what he was asking for. He wanted to see her do him. She also knew why. More than a month ago, she had two sex tapes to leak. The first was with Carlos while the second was with Jay. Kane was the only sexual partner she had who didn't have an intimate moment recorded. He now wanted one. It was the last thing she wanted to do, but she trusted him. She knew he would keep the recording private.

Carmen got up and went to the bathroom. She turned the light on, leaving the door cracked, so it wouldn't illuminate the whole room. Her cell phone then became propped on the dresser where it began to record.

She mounted him again except this time they were completely naked. They talked about having sex for weeks. At times, the opportunity was there, but they would stop themselves. Now, there wasn't anything standing in the way. Not even their own conscience.

"You like that," she asked him. She rubbed her clitoris over his manhood, wanting him to feel how wet she had gotten. When he moaned in response, she slipped his penis inside her. That move made him grab her hips. She placed her hands over his to remind him she was in control. She upped her speed, rocking back and forth over his dick as it stiffened. When he became fully erect, she took off like a madwoman. After the fourth expletive out his mouth, she smiled. "See, you can't even handle it," she joked. She slowed down for a bit, moving his hands from her hips to her breasts. She used it for leverage as she took off again.

The California King was strong, but the frame and headboard notified anyone in the house of what they were doing. She didn't even care. *I got something else.* She recalled a move she saw Jas do. She shifted her body, so she was at an angle, and rode him at full throttle. The move made his eyes roll in the back of his head. It also stimulated her clit ten times over. She felt herself on the verge of release. The feeling escalated when Kane's dick jerked inside her. She immediately came, her body falling on top of his.

He used it to his advantage. When he sucked her nipple; she came a second time. That orgasm lingered longer than the first. "Did you like it?" she moaned. His mouth was still occupied. "Tell me you liked it." He ran his fingers through her hair before pulling her face towards him. Their lips connected for minutes on end. After what felt like an hour, she repeated her question.

Kane described the experience with four words. "You're my wife now."

TEN

It didn't take long for Kane's statement to become a stamp. It started when Salazar's product swept through the clubs. It grew when the product hit lounges and cigar bars. With the name Kong being whispered around the city, Kane wanted to give it a face. The Vegas nightlife became their playground. Always at his side, their clientele, club owners, bottle girls, bouncers, and the like, referred to Carmen as Kong's wifey.

It was a title she didn't confirm or deny. Even under the guise of Karma Levy, she was still a married woman and a public figure. Carmen could count on one hand the number of times someone recognized her. Or at least the number of times someone told her they recognized her. It worked to her benefit that there were only a handful of Flame stores on the West Coast. The name Carmen Davenport was all over the brand, but she wasn't the face of any of her collections. If someone called her Carmen or said she favored the fashion designer for Flame, she would joke that she got that all the time. Even Floyd, if he were around, would help sway people.

If she were on the East Coast, things would be different. She was recognizable everywhere she went. Since she did most of her dirt in New York, she was always on the front page of *The Brookstone Times* and on her hometown's local news stations. Her plate was clean in Las Vegas, so her image remained absent from the pages of *The Las Vegas Review-Journal* and *The Las Vegas Sun*. In terms of a national level, Carmen was lucky that most people she crossed paths with on the Vegas club scene weren't readers of *Vogue*, *InStyle*, or *Elle*.

She did make a name for herself when her sex tapes leaked, but once the next Hollywood scandal hit, she was no longer the talk of the town. On the West Coast, she was like John Cato, Ralph Lauren, Tom Ford, and Mickey Drexler. Fashion designers and CEOs whose brands were famous, but if they were to walk in a grocery store or movie theater, most people wouldn't know who they were.

The title of Kong's wifey became hard to shake with how fast Kane was moving. Since she'd never been a drug user, she didn't know how good Salazar's product was. When club and bar hours no longer sufficed their clientele, Kane was forced to put the product on the streets. That was where

Felix and his crew came in. Their short stint in the Santiago cartel taught them well. They knew which places in Vegas and LA to hit.

Carmen stayed away from that part of the operation, playing the role she was stamped. She took care of the house, making sure it was clean and a cooked meal was readily available. She also took care of Kane, satisfying him two or three times a day if needed. The money came and he handled his business. Salazar was happy, Jas and Floyd were satisfied, and his crew reaped the benefits of their work. She also saw a payday as well. The money was great, yet the stability in her and Kane's relationship was even greater. Long gone were the arguments and crying spells.

Then, she came home to a cherry red Jaguar in the driveway. The car opened her eyes. She found it perfectly acceptable for them to splurge on clothes, but a luxury vehicle shouldn't have been in the equation. Not when there was an Escalade and Mercedes Benz in the driveway. Too busy living in the world of Kong, they forgot about their reality. They still didn't know where Dumati was and there weren't any leads. They hadn't even cracked the code on the package Kane found at Cohiba.

"What's that outside?" That was the first thing out her mouth.

Kane was sitting in the living room, a bottle of Cîroc in his hand. The movie, *A Bronx Tale*, played on the TV. "A gift," he replied.

"A gift for me or a gift for you?"

"If it's a gift for me, it's a gift for you."

His response made her drop her purse on the counter. She reminded herself he was drinking. His words could've been nothing but alcohol talking. She grabbed the bottle from his hand and set it on an end table. "Did you buy that car?"

"I said it was a gift." He grabbed her arm and pulled her in his lap. "Where were you?"

She could smell the alcohol on his breath. He knew where she was. It was the same place she went every Friday night. Most times with him. They hung out at La Zona Roja, keeping an eye on their product and the clientele. "Time for bed." She stood up from his lap, pulling his arm with her. "We're gonna get you showered, then under the covers." He didn't move from the couch, causing her to pull his arm again. When she did, her phone rung from the kitchen. "One second."

She raced to get it, taking the bottle of Cîroc with her. A number she didn't know was displayed on her burner phone. Instead of ignoring it, she answered.

"Is the offer still good?" a male voice asked.

Carmen didn't know who she was talking to. "What offer?"

"Damn, didn't you hunt me down?" The man had an attitude. "Now, you don't know me?"

"Oh my gosh, Brick. It's been like what, a month?"

"I heard about Kong," he told her. "He's makin' some moves out here. Put me on."

Carmen sighed. Both she and Kane thought they'd washed their hands of Brick when they didn't hear from him. With Kane's current state, it wasn't the best time to tell him he popped up. "Give me a day or two. I gotta ease you on him. Is this your best number?"

"It's my only number."

"Cool, I'll give you a call." Carmen hung up the phone. She went back to Kane and helped him to his feet. His tipsiness had her suspicious as he rarely drunk.

"How's the kids?" he asked as they climbed the stairs.

The question made her curse. She didn't know how her kids were. At least not two of them. Every time she called, Fiona and Silvas would feed her an excuse as to why Rakim and Nyla couldn't come to the phone.

"They have it. I gave it to them," Fiona would say. "I made sure it was charged before they went to the hospital. They play their games on it. Maybe it died." Silvas would echo something similar. She would then ask him to pass the kids his phone and he would feed her another excuse.

"Kristian took them to the café for a snack. Call her."

She would follow whatever path they sent her down. The call would always end with her not speaking to them. Yesterday, she broke. She cursed Fiona out and accused her of keeping her children from her. She even told her she was fired. Those words sent Fiona into a fit of tears.

"You don't know what I'm dealing with." Fiona's voice elevated to new heights. "I'm doing the best that I can. Guillermo and Señora aren't here anymore. They went back to Puerto Rico. I don't have any extra help. I'm sorry. I'm doing the best that I can."

She yelled something in Spanish, which Carmen couldn't understand. What she could understand was Fiona's pain. "I'm sorry, too." Carmen told Fiona to forget what she said. "I know you wouldn't do anything to hurt me. I just miss my babies."

Fiona accepted the apology.

Carmen blinked her eyes. She was now standing in front of the walk-in shower. Kane was inside butt-naked, his face towards the shower floor. "Why were you drinking like that?" She rubbed the back of his neck. "That's not like you." She rubbed his neck some more.

He raised his head towards hers. "Has your mind changed about us?"

There went a question she didn't expect. "What do you mean?"

"We're together. You keep tellin' me you love me."

Carmen took a step back from the shower. "I do love you. I would never lie about that."

"Do you see us getting married again?"

She headed towards the sink to analyze the question. *Why is he asking me that? He knows I'm not leaving Jay.* The question was delicate, one she couldn't rush to answer. After some time, she found the right reply. "Right now, that's not an option. If it were to become one, I would consider it."

"Would Jay have to die for it to be?"

Carmen faced him. "Why would you ask me that?" She waited for a response. When she didn't get one, she left the room. He wanted to discuss marriage when they never talked about putting it on the table. It was like someone had gotten in his ear.

I'll figure it out, she thought. *I always do. Something is up.*

***

Unlike other mornings, the Las Vegas heat didn't wake Carmen up. This time, it was the tickle of a forest-like scent in her nostrils. Not sure what it could be, she sniffed the air as her eyes flickered open. The first thing she saw was the black rolling tray in Kane's lap. *That's not what I think it is.* She watched as he finished rolling a blunt, then lit it. *Is this happening?* She sat up in bed right as he put the blunt to his lips. He took a long drag before blowing the smoke out his mouth.

Once again, she was questioning who he was. It seemed like every day that passed, she was seeing more of Kong than of Kane. The Kane she married didn't smoke. The man in front of her, not only smoked, he knew how to roll a blunt.

It shocked her, but what shocked her even more was how turned on she was by it. There was a sexiness about the way he emitted the smoke from his mouth. It made him appear more rugged. If that was who Kong was supposed to be, Kane was playing the hell out the role. She was even getting caught up.

Carmen didn't tell him to stop, but she moved the rolling tray to a dresser. Her hands then pulled back the rim of his plaid boxers. Lust and temptation were dancing in the air like the smoke. The more she sucked, the more smoke he blew.

"Right there, baby," she heard him mutter. "Right there." He held her head in his lap. "Right there," he moaned. When the grunts came, so did the explosion. She held his nut in her mouth, continuing to suck him off a few seconds longer.

You better bring up Brick now, a voice said in her head. *You got him in a good mood.*

Carmen released his manhood from her hands. She set her head in his lap, swallowing his seed. She peered at him; his eyes dimmed from the high. "Brick called me last week."

"You gonna suck me off and then say that?" He reached across the bed for the rolling tray. He set his blunt in it. "What did he want?"

"Well, you know your name is in the streets. He wants in."

Kane picked his blunt back up. "I need another man, but it ain't gonna be him. I'm meeting with Salazar tonight to re-up."

Carmen almost jumped on him. "Are you fuckin' crazy?"

"We need more time to find Dumati."

"You re-upping has nothing to do with Dumati," Carmen shrieked. "Salazar trusts you. Get in there and ask some questions. Don't get any more shit you gotta sell."

"He's having a pool party tonight," Kane said, overlooking her comment. "Wear something sexy. Keep up the façade. Me and the guys will be handling business."

"So now you like being here?"

Kane set her straight. "I like being with you. Don't get it twisted."

Carmen almost said something they knew was a lie. She was going to tell him they could be together in Brookstone, but that wasn't the truth. The second they were back in New York, they were back to being ex-husband and ex-wife. "We can't get caught up."

"Caught up in what?" Kane gave her a death stare. "If you're talking about Salazar, I'm not telling you what I want, I'm telling you what's happening. If you're talking about us, baby, we're there. We ain't just fuckin' to fuck. We're together. Ain't that why you put my name on the house?"

"I'm married."

He shrugged his shoulders at that response. "On paper."

She couldn't even say she was surprised. Why would anyone believe she was married with the way she was carrying on? Her husband was miles away, fighting for his life, and she was spending her morning sucking off her ex. *This is about to bite me in the ass. I'm to blame for him being like this.* "You don't need to re-up."

"I appreciate your concern."

Those words made her get out the bed. Without another word to him, she showered and dressed. She didn't even tell him when she invited Brick over. She allowed Kane to see him when he came downstairs. Kane didn't look pleased, but neither was she. Brick was her payback for his decision to re-up.

"You need an extra hand, right?" She said it to tick him off. Kane didn't respond. All he did was open the fridge and pull out a bottle of orange juice. He took it to the living room, leaving her and Brick in the kitchen.

"You didn't tell him I was coming?" Brick whispered.

"He doesn't tell me everything," she whispered back.

"Look, if he ain't open to having a conversation then why am I here?"

"To make him open," Carmen replied.

Brick took those words as his invitation. He headed towards the living room. Carmen didn't follow him, choosing to watch from a distance. He shared words with Kane, but it was obvious her ex wasn't bending. Brick returned, shaking his head. "Thanks for trying. I'll get in my way."

"What did he say?" Carmen wanted specifics.

"That same ol' bullshit he's always talkin'. Don't worry about it. I can get some work somewhere else."

"If Salazar didn't let you in, why should I?" Kane yelled from the living room. "I know you talked to him."

His words were reminiscent of what she'd been previously told by Jas. "Don't even argue with him," she whispered to Brick. "I'm sorry I got you into this."

"You can make it up to me," he proposed. "You ever ate at Bacchanal in Caesars Palace?"

"I have, but it's been awhile. Is that where you're headed?"

"Join me." Brick nodded towards Kane. "You'll have another way to make him mad."

Carmen smiled at how Brick caught on to her scheme. "Well, I didn't cook, so…" Her voice trailed off. "Let me get my purse." She did just that and when she returned, she was on Kane's radar. He met her at the door right as she was about to exit.

"You ain't going no—" she was quick to cut him off.

"Are you gonna ask him about Presi?"

Although her intention had nothing to do with the drug kingpin, it got her out the house. In terms of what she would face when she came back, that was a different story.

ELEVEN

The Bacchanal Buffet was a foodie paradise. It was the last place Carmen needed to be eating especially since she had to be half-naked at Salazar's party. As much as she told herself to eat light, it was the last thing she did. She returned to the table with two plates stacked high of the best brunch options known to man. "The salmon looks amazing. Have you tried it?" She looked at Brick's plate to see what he had. "Ooh, you got some."

Brick laughed at her antics. "Kong doesn't let you out much."

"He does. We go out together."

"My point," Brick replied. "Together." He stuck his fork inside the salmon, giving it a taste. "It's good. I may have to get seconds."

"You better get it now. We only have ninety minutes." She mentioned the restaurant's time policy on purpose.

"We do, don't we?"

The way he asked the question made Carmen feel as if something was coming.

"Tell me about yourself, Karma."

There it was. "Come on, we don't need to get personal," she began. "You saw how Kong was back there. This is the last time we're gonna see each other. Why get to know each other now?"

"You know you don't have to live like this."

Carmen set her fork down. She could tell from his tone, he was trying to play savior. She needed saving, but not from him or Kane. She needed it from herself. Lust and selfishness led her down a road she thought she'd never see again. "What you think my problem is, is not my problem. Kong isn't taking care of me because I'm sleeping with him. He's taking care of me because I'm his girl. Someone had to tell you I'm wifey."

"I'm not talking about you being a prostitute," Brick explained. "I'm talking about you being caught up in this game. You should get out while you can."

Carmen pointed her fork at him. "Didn't you come over so you can *get* in the game? Fuck off. Practice what you preach."

"We're two players with two very different motives."

She stuffed her mouth with more food, but that didn't stop her from talking. "Who are you? What's your motive? I'm still curious to know why you're here. You don't have family back in Jamaica? Isn't your job done?"

"That question again," Brick said with a chuckle. "Kong didn't go back either."

"But I know why he's here. Shit, I'm half the reason."

Brick chuckled. "He can get pussy anywhere."

"But not the pussy he wants," Carmen shot back. "I'm what he wants."

"He got your head so big. That's what happens when dudes start making hoes housewives."

Carmen threw a napkin roll-up at him. It hit him at the base of his neck before falling on the floor. "It's about what it is, not what it looks like. I was never a prostitute or in Salazar's harem. I hooked up with Jas and got more than I bargained for. Instead of trying to fuck me, Kong took the time to get to know me. He made a housewife a housewife."

"If that's what you want me to believe."

Brick stood up from the table. He told her he was going to get more salmon. If she were honest with herself, she shouldn't have cared about him calling her a hoe. She couldn't fault him for what he thought because that's what he saw. She was introduced to him as a sex worker although she was far from it. If she didn't play it smart, she would blow her own cover.

Well, what kind of timing is this?

Lownes' number appeared on her phone. It had been a week or two since she last talked to him. She needed to answer because she needed to tell him about Kane. The only thing stopping her was Brick. He hadn't returned, which meant she couldn't leave the table. When he reappeared, the call was going to voicemail.

"Excuse me," she told Brick, getting up. "Kong called," she fibbed. "I gotta take this."

Brick said something to her, which she didn't make out. She hurried out the restaurant, dialing Lownes number as she went. The hotel was packed, but she was able to find a quiet corner with minimal guests. "You gotta help me," she told him. "Kane is trying to re-up."

"He's trying to do what?"

She filled Lownes in. It wasn't the best thing to do since he and Kane weren't on good terms, but she needed advice on how to stop him. "You know we haven't gotten anywhere. Salazar trusts him, but that's not getting us what we want."

"Nah, it's delaying it," Lownes said. "If you ask me, Kane is doing the re-up for himself. Like I told you before, Kane's original idea would've had y'all in and out. He should've taken the bricks to the Triad and planned the raid. The only good thing coming out the route y'all went is that y'all know Salazar's house. Every time Kane goes over there, I know he's taking notes. That knowledge is gonna make it easier for him to take Salazar down."

"How do I stop him?" she asked.

"You leave," was Lownes' response. "You're the only taste of home he has. You told me he said he likes being with you. That's why he's re-upping. He wants to go back to Brookstone, but he doesn't want to go back to the life he had with you. The more shit he gotta sell, the longer he gets to have you on his arm. If you leave, I promise you, Carm, he's gonna snap out of it. Let's keep it real. You've told me in so many words that y'all are sleeping together. Take your pussy and leave. Trust me, Ma, the dick will follow."

Carmen heard him loud and clear. She did need to leave. If she took a break, even if it were for three days, she would get a chance to see her kids and Jay. "What do I do if that plan doesn't work? He may shock us both."

"He ain't gonna shock us." There was a slight chuckle in Lownes' voice. "Go home. I promise you. He'll be right behind you. What's gonna happen is y'all are gonna get a clear head. When y'all come back, it's going to be all about Dumati. Y'all may not even fuck this round."

Carmen checked the hall to make sure Brick wasn't lurking. When she saw the way was clear, she continued the conversation. "I'm gonna talk to him again. If he's still trying to re-up, I'll go to the pool party, but I'll leave right after. I'll be on the first flight to New York in the morning."

"If you gotta come home, take a picture of that package. We'll work on trying to decode the numbers while you're here. At least when you go back, you'll have something figured out."

"I will," Carmen replied. With a plan in place, she felt more confident than before. Regardless of what Kane did, she was going to keep the investigation moving. They had been in Vegas too long without anything to show for it.

***

Not once did Carmen think about what she was going to find when she walked in the house. The only thing she thought about was what she was going to say when Kane asked her about Brick. Since she prepared for the latter, she was surprised to find Kane with his head in his hands. He looked like something was bothering him. If it was her breakfast with Brick, she succeeded at her plan. If it was something else, her head was about to be in her hands, too.

"Would you like me to make you something?" She started there to shape the mood. He shook his head. Certain something was wrong, she joined him on the steps. "Do you—" she couldn't get the words out as he spoke over her.

"I've been fuckin' up for a while now," he told her. "I didn't even want to be here this long." He took his head out his hands. "I'm gonna do better, I promise. I'm gonna get us out of here." He ran his hand through her hair. "I'm not gonna re-up. I'll tell Salazar tonight. Tomorrow, I'll go to the Triad office. I'll talk to the team and get something moving."

Lownes was right and wrong at the same time. She didn't even have to go to Brookstone for Kane to wake up. All she had to do was leave the house with Brick. "I'm glad you changed your mind," she told him. "I think it's time we both start making better decisions. This is the first one." She brought his hand to her lips. "This means a lot to me. I know it won't be easy turning him down. You made him a lot of money."

"*We* made him a lot of money," Kane corrected. "You had the club hook-up."

She kissed his hand again. "We," she agreed.

He pulled his hand from hers, but only so he could grab her face. He held her head alongside his. "I wouldn't have made it without you," he whispered. He brushed his lips against her cheek before separating from her. "What did you learn about Presi?"

"Nothing," she told him. "Brick knows how to keep his mouth shut. He did try and play savior on me. You know he gotta look out for a sista."

Kane chuckled. "Did he give you a Protect Black Women speech? Or did he go Salazar's route and tell you Black women are the mothers of civilization?"

"Neither." Carmen stood up. "Are you sure you don't want me to cook anything? I can order out if you'd prefer that."

"I wanna go for a drive. I think it'll help me sort some things out."

"Okay, well, I'll give you some time to yourself." Carmen kissed his forehead. "I'll be here." She walked up a few steps. Kane hadn't moved, but by the time she reached the top of the stairwell, she heard him getting up. Her initial plan was to pick out a swimsuit for the party. What ended up happening was the exact opposite. The moment she walked in their bedroom, she collapsed on the bed, now overcome with fatigue.

TWELVE

Salazar's mansion didn't look like the setting for a drug deal. It looked exactly like what it was supposed to be—a pool party. People were everywhere, drinking, smoking, living their best life or at least that was the visual at the pool. In Carmen's opinion, it worked to Kane's benefit he wasn't re-upping. If he hadn't changed his mind, he would've been stopped every two minutes by a drunk partygoer questioning him about boxes. A re-up also wouldn't have limited their time at the party. Carmen only had to play nice long enough for Kane to have a conversation.

I really don't, Carmen thought, *but I might as well have fun while I'm here.*

Everyone at the pool looked like they were in their early or mid-twenties. Carmen was double their age, but her parents' good genes and God's favor allowed her to look like she wasn't. She blended in with the crowd, wearing a white one-piece by the popular LA brand, *Mint Swim*. She paired it with her diamond studded stilettos, which she took off before draping her legs in the pool.

A DJ was set up in the backyard, spinning a song Akaila used to keep on repeat called, "Work from Home." She bopped to it until her presence caught Jas' attention. She was dressed like Carmen would've expected. A tiny nude bikini bottom bled into her skin along with a matching buckle bikini top. She brought three other girls with her who Carmen recognized from the line-up and the club. "Nice," Carmen said, complimenting her suit.

"I would say the same, but I don't like the modesty." Jas brushed her hands across her chest. "Well, you got some titties out, so that'll do."

Jas grabbed her left breast and after a few seconds of playtime, Carmen moved her hand. She did it playfully as she knew Jas was still crushing on her. She hadn't fulfilled her promise to her and luckily, Jas hadn't pushed her.

Jas noticed her playtime was being cut short. "Is Kong here?"

"He's inside talking to Salazar," Carmen replied. She looked at the other girls Jas was with. None of them bothered to speak. They looked like they were in their own world. She realized they were when she noticed the white powdery substance in their hands. "I thought tonight was gonna be mellow."

"Here?" Jas questioned with a laugh. "Come on, Karma."

"How many times have I been over here for a party?"

"Not enough, because you still owe me one." Jas got fresh again sliding her hand inside the seat of her bathing suit. She fingered her for a few seconds before Carmen moved her hand.

"Damn, Karm. Kong ain't even around. Shit, I could've gone deeper."

"I want to be respectful," Carmen explained. "We had an agreement."

"Well, tell him to hurry up, so we can fuck."

It was the first time Jas brought up their deal. Carmen assumed it was because Kane wasn't there. If he was at the pool, Jas would've been on her best behavior. "I'll talk to… Shit," Carmen yelled, feeling someone splash her with water. The chlorine burned her eyes as screams sounded over the music. Unsure of what was happening, she rubbed her eyes until she regained her vision. When she did, Jas was struggling to pull a girl out the pool.

Carmen sprang into action, aware she was witnessing an overdose. She helped Jas pull the girl on the pool deck. Everyone else was standing around looking scared or were too stoned to know what was going on.

"Go inside and ask for Mija," Jas screamed. "Go."

Carmen didn't know who that was, but she did as Jas instructed. She ran inside the house looking for anyone she could find. The living room was empty, which was where she thought she would find Salazar and Kane. She ran in every room she could, screaming for help, until she ran into Martí. "A girl OD'd," she yelled, out of breath. "Jas told me to ask for Mija."

"Fuck," Martí mouthed.

He took off up the steps. Unsure of what she should do, Carmen ran outside. A crowd had gathered around. "Excuse me." Carmen pushed her way into the circle. "Martí is getting Mija."

"Well, where the fuck is she?" Jas roared. "She's fuckin' dyin'."

Carmen stared at the girl, seeing her eyes rolled back in her head. Her lips were also turning a faint purplish color. If she had knowledge on how to handle an overdose, she would've done more. Truth be told, if she wasn't at Salazar's house, she would've called 911.

"Move," someone yelled.

The voice wasn't directed at her, but Carmen grabbed her heels and got out the way. A woman in a pair of navy blue scrubs dropped to her knees before injecting something in the girl's veins. Although she didn't wear a nametag, evidence suggested she was Mija. Why Salazar had an on-call nurse, she didn't know, but if she wasn't there, the girl would've been in a body bag.

"Carry her upstairs," Mija said to Martí after a few minutes. "She'll be fine, but she may need another dose." Martí did as she said.

Jas followed him and Mija into the house as did Carmen. While Martí and Jas went in a room close to Salazar's, Mija went to a room at the far end of the hall.

"Karma." Carmen turned to find Martí's eyes on hers. "Stay with Jas."

She did as he asked, going inside the room where Jas was. She found her inside lying on the bed next to her friend who was regaining consciousness. "I'm glad Mija was here." Carmen touched Jas' hand. "Is she always here for these parties?"

Jas sniffled. "She's not here for this."

Carmen rubbed her lips together. "Is Salazar sick?"

"Look, don't worry about her." Jas brushed her off. "She's nobody, okay?"

Carmen knew Mija wasn't a nobody. Still, she decided not to probe. She remained quiet until Martí came back to the room. He told her Kong was ready to leave. "I can stay if you want me to," she told Jas. "I'll tell him what happened."

Jas told her no. "You'll only distract me. I need to be with her."

Carmen understood. She kissed Jas' cheek. Martí escorted her out like he knew she planned to check out the room down the hall. With the way Jas snapped at her, there was something about Mija she wasn't supposed to know. She made a mental note to ask Kane about her once they were alone. That plan was abandoned when she saw him. Felix and Jose were at his side, neither of them dressed for a pool party. "What's going on?" The two men greeted her but were quick to leave. "What's going on?" she repeated to Kane.

"Let's go," he barked.

She heard the doors unlock. She got inside, now even more suspicious. "Why were they here?" She spoke of Felix and Jose. Kane didn't respond, driving as if he didn't hear her. "Please don't give me the silent treatment. A girl OD'd tonight."

"I heard," was all she got out of him.

"What happened with Salazar?"

That question he ignored. He kept driving, giving her the silent treatment although she asked him not to. She looked behind her to see the backseat was empty. She then looked at him. She stared at him for a solid minute, but he never looked her way. *I guess I gotta figure this out myself.* Within seconds, she had her seatbelt off and was climbing in the backseat. That caught Kane's attention.

"What are you doing?"

It was now her turn to ignore him. He asked again, his voice now much louder. She didn't answer, continuing to look for a level or release that would let down the backseat. She had a feeling he'd reupped. For one, his conversation with Salazar lasted longer than if he'd declined. In addition, Felix and Jose wouldn't have been at the house. The next clue she got was when he pulled off the road. She hadn't succeeded in getting the seat down, but that was miniscule to him. In no time, he was in the backseat, pulling her out the car.

"What did you do?" She punched him in his shoulder. He dropped her on the ground. She made it to her feet, ducking past him to hit the trunk release button. He grabbed her to prevent her from going near the trunk when he should've been trying to close it. It took only seconds for her to see she was bamboozled. "You fuckin' liar," she screamed, noticing the boxes. She punched him again, this time hitting him square in the face.

"You fuckin' bitch," he yelled. He wrapped his hands around her neck, throwing her down into the backseat. "What I tell you about punchin' me?" Carmen tried to kick him in his groin. She didn't aim right, only kicking air. "Stop this shit. You got me out here lookin' crazy."

"Fuck you," Carmen retorted. "Fuck you."

He pushed her legs in the car and slammed the door. "This ain't your shit," he yelled, the engine coming back to life. "I move how I wanna move. I run this."

Her cries were her only response.

"Next time you punch me, I'm punchin' you in your fuckin' throat. You wanna hit me like a man. I'll whoop your ass like one. Then, I'll fuck you good after I do it."

Carmen cried harder. Nothing about him reminded her of the man she married twice.

"Your fuckin' husband slung drugs all up and down the fuckin' East Coast and what cha give him? Fuckin' babies. He got a fuckin' reward. Grimy ass muthafucka. Fucked my wife and got her pregnant. Got my next wife killed. You better pray I don't cross paths with him again. I'ma shoot him my got damn self." He didn't let up. "Punchin' me in my got damn face. If I punched you back, your whole shit would've been rocked." He paused for only a second. "Fuck," he yelled. He hit the steering wheel. "You're my fuckin' heart, yo. You're my fuckin' heart."

The ride home wasn't long. Still, Carmen's tears put her to sleep. When she woke, Kane was carrying her inside the house. He put her on the bed and the second he tried to undress her, she pushed him away. He begged her to talk. She refused. Instead, she followed Lownes' plan. She changed her clothes, packed a suitcase, and left.

It wasn't done that simply either. Kane stopped her many times. He begged, he pleaded. They tussled. A small grab here and there turned into pushing and pulling. His hands ripped her bathing suit. She tore his wifebeater to shreds. The night grew deep and dark. Chaotic insanity turned them into versions of themselves they didn't recognize.

Kane went into a hazy daze. His conscience shot, he didn't see his hands when he pinned her to the floor. He didn't feel his legs when they separated hers. Nor did he feel the wetness on his penis when he tried to penetrate her. What he did feel was her spit on his face. He felt the throbbing in his knuckles after he punched her. Then, came the tightness in his chest when she left.

That woke him up.

Thirteen

Carmen got a room for the night at Caesars Palace. She cried herself to sleep and when she woke around four, she pretended the previous night didn't happen. After booking a one-way flight to Brookstone, she called Lownes. She told him to give her a day or two and then they could get to work. He respected her wishes, knowing she needed to catch up with her family.

While the hospital was the first place she wanted to go, she went home. When she walked in her house, the first thing she noticed was the silence. It was too quiet. To make some noise, she dropped her suitcase in the middle of the foyer. What was supposed to be a thud sounded like a shatter. Her eyes danced around the space before becoming deadlocked on the dining room. Fiona's hands were in the air, tears in her eyes. A broken platter was at her feet along with the food that had been on it.

Carmen didn't care about the mess because she saw something else. For weeks she thought about what she would say to Jay when he woke up. She imagined she would kiss his lips, tell him she loved him, and hold him in her arms until she had to share him with the kids. That wasn't about to happen. What she was feeling was betrayal and manipulation. She knew from his doctors that if he woke up, he wouldn't immediately be released. "We won't let him come home for another two or three weeks," they told her. For him to be sitting in their dining room, he'd been awake for a while.

"You knew," she said to Fiona. Those words sent Fiona running in the kitchen crying. Carmen looked at Jay. *Why didn't he call her? Why didn't he say something?* She didn't always keep her phone on, but if he called, he would've gotten a response within forty-eight hours. He didn't even have to call her. Anyone in her village could've sent a smoke signal. None of them said anything.

She walked inside the dining room, giving him a once-over. He was sitting in his usual seat at the head of the table. She could only see him from mid-chest up. His hair was freshly cut, and he was shaven. Despite being groomed, the scowl on his face made him look rough. She didn't let it scare her away. She neared him until her foot hit something hard. When she peered down, she understood why no one said anything. He was sitting in a wheelchair.

She knew there was a possibility he could be paralyzed. She told herself it wouldn't matter. It didn't, but she was still shocked to see that was the case. Or so she thought. He slammed the palms of his hands on the table. He shook as he did it, but he managed to stand up. *He's not paralyzed.* She ran and grabbed him. She threw her arms around him, crying, telling him whatever came to mind. The sentiment wasn't returned. He pushed her off him.

Carmen backed away. Automatically, she thought of every sin she'd committed. "I can explain," she began. "I—" He didn't allow her to finish. He grabbed his glass of iced tea and threw it across the room. "I'm sorry," she told him. "I fucked up. It happened so fast."

His anger was directed elsewhere. "I woke up alone."

There she was, about to tell on herself, when he didn't even know about her infidelity.

"You weren't there," he continued. "My kids weren't there. I was fuckin' alone."

"Silvas was supposed to be sittin—"

"Silvas ain't my fuckin' wife." He spit out his words. "You were supposed to be there. Not in fuckin' Vegas. You let Kane handle that shit. You stay with your fuckin' husband."

"They didn't tell you?" Carmen was growing upset by the second. "I was there. I was wearin' your fuckin' blood. I was holding your hand, neglecting our kids, beggin', prayin', pleadin', cryin' out to God for you to come back. The only reason I left was to find the man who did this."

"If you didn't find him, it wasn't worth it. You shouldn't have been lookin' for him, anyway. It's a death sentence." He plopped down in his chair. "Tell Fiona to bring me my lunch." He wheeled himself out the dining room. He didn't go far, only across the hall, which is how she learned the home office wasn't an office anymore. It was a bedroom. There was also construction going on. A full bathroom was being built inside.

"I love you," she cried.

"I don't wanna hear that right now. Tell it to Rakim and Nyla. They're upstairs. I know they wanna see you. Oh, and congratulations. I heard you and Kane have a new baby."

"Don't." She pointed her finger at him. "Don't say anything about Bella."

He stood up from the chair. Although it took him a long time to do it, he walked towards her. He got as close to her as he could before giving her a stern, "Fuck you." That was enough to send Carmen out the room. She grabbed her luggage and headed up the steps. After showering and changing clothes, she headed to Rakim's room. She put on a happy face although she'd been crying her eyes out. The welcome she wished she got from Jay came from Rakim and Nyla. For hours, they hugged, kissed, shared giggles, and played games on Rakim's iPad.

When she ventured downstairs, Fiona was setting the table for dinner. Her maid uttered apologies left and right, explaining what Jay already told her. "We didn't want to do it, but he was so angry. We couldn't let you talk to Rakim and Nyla because they would've told you. He made us keep them from you." Fiona then shared that Jay woke up the night he moved his hand. "Silvas left to get a snack," she explained. "He wouldn't have left the room if he knew Jay was gonna wake up."

"Where is he now?" Carmen asked.

"He's with Kristian at Kane's condo. Bella had to come home. He's been helping over there. You know Arnold has the baby and Beverly." Fiona spoke of Kane's parents. Arnold needed the extra hands as Beverly was suffering from dementia.

Carmen realized how in the dark she was. "No one told me Bella was out the NICU. Kane didn't even mention it. I'm certain he knew." Right when she said those words, a new thought popped in her mind. Kane knew Jay was awake. She remembered when she came home to find him drinking. Up until that night, things had been smooth sailing. That night was the turning point. If he knew, his decision to re-up explained everything. He was doing it for the reason Lownes said, to keep her in Vegas with him. Unfortunately, his plan backfired.

"I'm headed to see Bella," Carmen announced. "I won't make it back for dinner. Put the food up and I'll fix a plate later." Fiona told her she would. Carmen left the house without even looking towards Jay's room. It wouldn't have mattered, anyway. The door was closed. She headed to Kane's condo, shocking everyone with her presence. After catching up with them and spending a few hours loving on Bella and Kristian, she returned home with Silvas in her passenger seat.

This time when she walked in the house, it was alive. Rakim and Nyla were in Jay's room, watching a movie. Not wanting to interrupt them, she headed towards the kitchen only to hear Jay tell Rakim he needed to talk to her.

"We'll finish the movie tomorrow after breakfast."

"But we wanna sleep in here," Rakim cried.

"I know," Jay told him. "Me and Mama gotta catch up. Tomorrow y'all can sleep with us."

To show Jay she heard him, she walked towards his room. She stood in the doorway, waiting for Rakim and Nyla to get out the bed. "Come on, guys. I know it's hard," she told them, "but y'all had him for a long time without me."

"Daddy rolled me around in his chair," Nyla screeched.

"It was part of my physical therapy," Jay explained.

"Well, now it's time for Daddy's verbal therapy." Carmen walked inside the room and offered the kids her hands. "Daddy and I gotta talk about Bella. I know y'all want to see her more."

Nyla squealed. "Mrs. Beverly says she looks like Kristian as a baby."

"She does," Carmen agreed. She reached for Nyla and pulled her towards her. She did the same with Rakim. Once she got them out the bed, it was easier to get them up the stairs. In no time, she had them tucked in. When she came back down, she prayed to God her conversation with Jay would go better than the one earlier. She closed the door behind her, in the event it didn't. "If the circumstances were different," she began, "I would've made the decision about Bella with you. I couldn't."

Jay's voice was calm. "You know I want another baby. I know she isn't biologically yours, but you're sharing an experience with Kane you know I want. Who am I to her? Am I her stepfather or just her mother's husband? Did y'all talk about that? This shit goes deep, Peaches." He called her by her childhood nickname.

"Bella is innocent in all this," he continued. "I don't have a problem with the baby. My problem is with Kane. It will always be with Kane. I played that card before. I tried to use Nyla to win you back." While their daughter was conceived after her divorce from Kane, Carmen gave birth to Nyla after she and Kane remarried. There were instances where Jay would fly to Puerto Rico only to call and request for her to bring Nyla to the island. On one of those visits, he let it be known he wanted sex. After she turned him down, he kicked her out the house. "He's gonna do the same. I know he is. He ain't got a wife no more. He's gonna look at you as available pussy."

There was a moment of silence. "The only reason I even mentioned Bella is because I was hurt," he admitted. "A lot of what I said to you was hurt. I thought your face was gonna be the first one I saw. I wanted it to be. In a way, I dreamt it. No one was there, and I lost it. I was alone for ten minutes, but it felt like ten years."

"I wanted the same." Carmen moved closer to him, sitting on the bed. She didn't comment on what he said about Kane as his worst fears had already come to light. "Do you support me being a mother to Bella? Can she be a part of our family?"

Jay's voice was still calm. "I would never say no to you being a mother. I know what it's like to lose one. I don't want that for any—" He stopped talking as his next set of words was contradictory. He was now aware of what happened to Patricia. Carmen knew he was the one who killed her mother. He also knew from his visits with their half-sister, Eleise, that she and Carmen had met. "I'm sorry," he told her. "I kept a lot from you. I was trying to protect you. I'm sorry."

"I know you are." Carmen squeezed his hand. She got up from the bed about to make her exit.

"That's it?"

Carmen looked behind her. "For right now, yes. I do want to talk about Dumati, but not tonight. Maybe in the morning."

"You haven't even touched me."

Carmen stifled a giggle. "I tried to give you a hug, remember?"

"That's not what I'm talking about, Carm."

Carmen raised her brow as she caught on. Sex was the last thing on her mind especially when her legs had been wide open for Kane for over a month. Nevertheless, she couldn't use that as an excuse. Her only two choices were to give in or argue. Then, a third came to mind. "Can you handle it?" she asked, thinking of his physical condition. "I don't wanna hurt you."

Jay chuckled. "Well, I can't do the tricks I used to, but I think I can handle a ride."

"This is a totally different vibe from earlier."

"I'm sorry about that," Jay replied. "I am. Can we forget that happened and start over?"

"So, fuck you should mean something different now?"

Jay pulled his T-shirt off, taking his wifebeater with it. With his chest on full display, she was able to see the scars of his gunshot wounds. The bullet holes took her back to that night. It was a nightmare she thought she wouldn't wake from.

"Do you still find me attractive?"

His question crushed her. At the same time, it made her want to touch him. Yes was an easy word to say, but it needed action. It was better to show than tell. She stripped down to her bra and panties. She straddled him, running her fingertips along his chest until she felt the wounds. Each one was met with a kiss, the words, "I love you," whispered in between. Then, she took the kisses from his chest to his lips. His legs might not have been the strongest, but there wasn't anything weak about his dick. She could feel its hardness.

While she always left him satisfied, she wanted to please him more than anything. It was the reason she pulled down her panties. When he went for her bra, she removed it, too, before reaching for his joggers. "I got chu," she told him. "Lay back." He did as she said, but when she kissed his lips, he tried to rush things. She tapped his hand before grabbing his penis into hers. "I said I got chu." She played with it for a bit before sliding it inside.

Like she did Kane, she started slow. She didn't want to put too much pressure on him since his legs were already holding her weight. When his hands grabbed her hips, it told her he could handle more. She gave it to him, rocking over his manhood how he liked.

"I may cum early," he warned.

That didn't matter. To show him, she picked up the pace. She still wasn't at full speed, nor had she done the move she learned from Jas. If he came before she could, he would get it another day. Thankfully, that didn't happen. By the time she got to it, he was still in the game. Hard as a fuckin' rock, but he hadn't exploded. She was about to make him, though. She sat on him at an angle and rode him sideways. She was five seconds in when he stopped her. He looked in between them then back at her. She waited for him to say something. Words didn't come, but he moved his hands from her hips as if to say continue.

That was the last interruption. She went full speed, watching as he bit his lip from the pleasure. "See how wet you make me," she whispered. She closed her eyes, feeling his lips on her nipple. She held his head to her chest, the sensations intensifying the harder he sucked.

"Fuck," he grunted.

Carmen closed her eyes when she felt his seed trickle down her inner thigh. For the first time in years, she hadn't cum with him. She could tell he noticed because right after he pulled out, he brushed the tip of his penis against her clit. In no time, she lost control. It was a rapid fall into a sea of bliss her spirit needed more than her body. That was why she didn't deny him hours later.

He woke her, whispering he needed more. She gave it to him and when she put him to sleep the second time, she didn't nod off. Thoughts of Dumati, Salazar, and red diamonds filled her head. Then, she remembered something. Jay told her a long time ago his private diamond collection was in a vault inside their home in San Juan. Since Dumati was his supplier, his packages had to look like the one from Cohiba. If she found one, there was a chance she could figure out what the serial numbers meant.

Anxious to do so, when five o'clock rolled around, she left the bed. She purchased a one-way ticket to San Juan and repacked her suitcase. After planting a kiss on a sleeping Rakim and Nyla, she took an Uber to the airport. Guilt traveled with her. Once again, Jay would wake up alone. To deal with it, she sent him a text saying she loved him, but had to find Dumati. She could've saved herself a trip and asked him about the packages, but she didn't want to run the risk of him being tightlipped. With the house at her disposal, she could get the answers she needed.

Upon reaching the basement door, she unlocked it with the code Jay gave her after their wedding. It was dark inside, but after she took two steps forward, the entire basement was lit. The vault was easy to find as its gold door stood out amongst the basement's ash-colored walls.

Getting inside, not so much. The passcode was a total of eleven digits and/or letters. That meant it could've been a combination of a name, a birthday, an address, etc. The first thing she tried was Jay's name as it had exactly eleven letters. The door beeped, letting her know she was wrong. *That takes out a lot of names because Santiago is eight letters itself.* She started to try her name until she realized the e in her middle name, Denise, would be the twelfth input.

Call Jay, a voice said in her head. *Ask him for the code. Tell him you won't take anything.*

"Please," she said aloud. "He's not giving me the code to his vault. Not when I've stolen from him." Carmen touched the keypad. Her index finger randomly landed on the number seven. P, Q, R, and S were the letters under the number. "P-I-N-K-S-U-N-R-I-S-E." She counted out the letters. "Eleven," she whispered. She inputted it and listened as the doors unlocked. She closed her eyes, giving God a prayer of thanks. She then opened the door and like the basement, the lights came on as she walked in.

Aside from the gray oval table in the center of the room, the vault contained nothing but safe deposit boxes. Just her luck, she didn't need a key to open them. One pull of the knob and each box was at her disposal. She only had to open two before she found what she was looking for. She pulled out a package right as her cell phone rung. When she saw Jay's picture on the screen, it reminded her it was the fifth time he was calling. To put his mind at ease, she texted him.

I will tell you everything in due time. I love you.

She went back to the package. The mailing label had Jay's name printed on it followed by the physical address of Flame. What made it useful was that the mailing label was taped over a series of handwritten numbers. She could only see two of the numbers, but it was there.

Using one of her keys, she tried to lift the tape to get the mailing label off. It took several tries, but once she got it going, it came up. Like the package at Cohiba, there were three rows of numbers. Since she had the printed mailing label, she could easily compare it to the serial numbers. In less than two seconds she saw Brookstone's five-digit zip code. It was the last five digits in the third row. The series of numbers was an address.

She grabbed her phone and pulled up the picture she'd taken of the package from Cohiba. She wrote out the numbers on the back of an old receipt. Then, using the keypad on her phone, she worked on decoding it. The first row was the hardest as she expected the package to be addressed to Alejandro Salazar. The first number was four, which meant she had to pick from the letters, G, H, and I. Once she spelled out, ISH, the rest was a breeze.

47462357252927

ISHMAEL SALAZAR

562737833929

56 CRESTED WAY

5278342789135

LAS VEGAS, 89135

The address to Salazar's house was 56 Crested Way. More than likely, that was the truck's next destination. Based off the package's addressee, it was also where Dumati was living. She knew from Kane he was Afro-Cuban. She assumed it was his nationality. According to his name on the package, that was only half true. He was Afro-Cuban because he was born of an African mother and a Cuban father by the name of Alejandro Salazar. Something told her his parents were never married and Dumati was his mother's last name.

Black women are the mothers of civilization.

Carmen took a breath.

"She's not here for this," was what Jas said about Mija. Carmen backed away from the table. Every time she went in Salazar's house, the very person she was looking for was inside. She remembered the door Mija went into. Evidence suggested it was Dumati's bedroom. After leaving The Ave, he flew to Vegas. Salazar's house was the only place he could go to stay hidden from the Triad. His father also had the financial means to provide him with private home care.

Another thought came to mind. Salazar never questioned Kane about the red diamonds. If he were expecting the package, he would've said something. Especially when Kane told him he stole his drugs. For some reason, Dumati didn't tell his father about the diamonds. Her suspicions told her their relationship was strained. She wouldn't be shocked if Dumati felt his father would steal from him. That thought made her dial Lownes' number.

"I need you," she told him once he answered. "Buy a ticket to Vegas."

After she explained her findings, she followed her own directive and bought a one-way ticket to Sin City. She then made another call. When the line picked up, she got down to business.

"I found a way for you to come home."

FOURTEEN

Kane could count on one hand the worst days of his life. The first was when he found out Carmen was pregnant by Jay with Rakim. The second was the day of the paternity trial when she learned he lied about being Rakim's father. A year prior to that day, Kane paid a fellow Triad agent to alter his DNA results to show he was Rakim's biological father versus Jay. Next came the night at the hospital when a Triad agent told him Monifah was one of the fifteen victims at The Ave.

The most recent was the night before last when Carmen left him. He could admit his conscience wasn't there. He blacked out. Everything he did was disgusting and undeserved. The same words could describe the way Carmen repaid him. Since she left, he cried, prayed, and thought about ways to get her back. Nothing sounded good enough. There wasn't anything he could buy because she could afford the riches he couldn't. She also wasn't going to listen to his apologies. He screamed them at her when she locked him out the bathroom. He crawled to her on his knees as she left, begging for forgiveness. None of it worked. The only thing he could do was fly home. His plan was to pick up Bella and drive to her house. He hated to use his daughter as a pawn, but with Bella in his arms, he had a greater chance of getting Carmen to talk to him.

Then, she called him. He didn't know where she was neither could he tell when he answered. He could hear her breathing, but other than that, the line was silent. It stayed that way for five minutes. He knew why, too. *What words could be said?* I'm sorry couldn't suffice for what either one of them did. It wouldn't remove her saliva that dripped from his nose. Nor would it take back the blow he gave to her head. Or what caused it all, the burning desire he had for her in his loins.

"I'm three feet away from a G19," he finally said. "Tell me why I shouldn't use it." Her breathing became louder. "Tell me why I shouldn't blow my fuckin' brains out."

"So I won't have to blow out mine."

A tear welled up in his eye. "I don't know what happened. I mean, I know what happened, but how we, how I, how it got that far. I don't know. I fucked up."

"We both fucked up," she told him. "It's not all on you and will never be. We both went off the cliff. What matters right now is if we want to grab hands so we can land together."

Her words gave him the comfort he was seeking. It told him the night was a wound they could heal. All that mattered is that they wanted to. He closed his eyes and prayed aloud to God. He repented for his transgressions, he prayed for peace and asked for strength. Minutes in, she prayed with him. They spoke to God together. Then, Carmen told him she was outside. That statement made him ask her if she'd gone home. When she said, yes, his face dropped.

"You knew Jay was awake, didn't you?"

In Kane's opinion, it didn't matter if he knew. The name of who told him didn't matter either. What mattered is that the day was there. The day he had to let her go.

"When we were in my garage, we had an entire conversation before we touched," Carmen said. "We didn't want to hurt each other. I thought being upfront would make it easier, but it's not. Like you gotta let me go, I gotta let you go, too. It's not one-sided."

Her tears told him it wasn't. She was hurting, too. Her hurt just couldn't compare to his. He grieved their marriage until he found Monifah. His new wife was a band aid on a gunshot wound. He lost the band aid, bled out, until Carmen sewed him up. Now, she was removing the stitches although his body hadn't healed.

"I love you so much," she cried, "but we have to do what's right."

Kane wanted to ask her if she said the same thing to Jay. How did she tell him she was ending their affair? Did she make Jay believe she would come back? Is that how Jay knew she would end up his wife? Kane wanted answers, but he chose not to ask. They were trying to salvage their relationship, not send it further in the gutter. Instead, he asked her to come inside. He thought they were ready to see each other. Carmen didn't. She needed more time. She then shared why she came back.

"All I'm asking for is a chance to get the girls out. They have nothing to do with what's going on. Let me see if I can get through to Jas."

"You have tonight," he replied. "I'm hittin' 'em in the morning."

"I'll take that."

The conversation didn't end there. They spoke for another hour before the call was disconnected. It took another thirty minutes before Carmen grabbed her luggage and headed in the house. The call broke the ice, but it didn't stop them from crying in each other's arms. It didn't stop the apologies or keep them from asking again for forgiveness. It only made it easier to do.

Once things were calm, Carmen took another shower. She changed into a dress that didn't scream Karma. It screamed Carmen which is who she was.

"I hope you didn't wear that for me," was the first thing out Jas' mouth. Carmen found her in the club's dressing room, applying her makeup.

"I don't want to see anything I can't touch," Jas added.

"Well, you don't have to look at me," Carmen joked. "I only need you to listen." She put her back towards the mirror, not wanting to see her own reflection. "This isn't easy for me to say. I need to say it, though." She paused to give her words a chance to sink in. "The bond we created was built on a lie."

"Oh, please, Danika told me the first day we met you had money."

Carmen peered at Jas. "Did she tell you how I made my money?"

"No, but does it matter?" Jas powdered her nose.

"My name is Carmen. I'm the CEO of Flame, Inc. My husband is Jay Santiago."

"Wait, wait, wait." Jas stood from her seat. "You're married?"

"Ishmael Dumati tried to murder my husband back in New York. I'm telling you this because the Triad is raiding Salazar's house tomorrow. You and the girls need to leave tonight. Y'all need to get out of Vegas. I don't care where you go, but you don't want to be near that house."

"This was a game to you?" Jas' voice was sharp.

"It was never a game. I was a woman with a motive."

Jas scoffed. "It was a game. Well, this ain't a game for me. Some of us ain't got shit but this."

"Don't chu know you can have more? You can't swing from a pole the rest of your life."

"Says the woman who never had to."

The mother in Carmen grabbed Jas' face. "I see something in you even if you don't see it in yourself. I'm trying to help. If you and the girls don't leave tonight, you'll be arrested tomorrow. They will find any and everything to stick you with."

Jas snatched her hand off her face. "Find someone else to save."

"Are you that loyal to him?"

"Compared to who?" Jas yelled. "To you? Salazar never lied to me. He showed me who he was from the jump. Do you think we would've gone that far if I knew you were married? Yeah, I would've done a little extra for some coins, but not that. Women like you think strippers are the bottom of the barrel, but some of us got morals."

Carmen tried to reason with her. "I apologize for not telling you the truth. I want to make it up to you. I can fly you anywhere in the world."

"Fly yourself to hell and we'll be squared away."

Jas bumped her as she left. Carmen followed behind her until Jas headed towards the stage. She stayed for her dance, trying again to reason with her once it was over. Jas didn't want to hear it. When she called for one of the club's bouncers, Carmen gave up. Or at least temporarily.

FIFTEEN

Carmen never mentioned to Kane she was stopping by Salazar's house. It hadn't been a part of the plan until she saw how Jas reacted. With the clock ticking, she tried one more time to get through to her. When Martí answered the door, she told him she came to see Jas.

"Why didn't you go to the club?" was the first question out his mouth.

"I did," she replied. "We spoke, but we need to speak again."

"Why did you think she was here if you left her at the club?"

Martí was interrogating her like she didn't have her story together. Thankfully, the one she was giving was the truth. "I saw her when she left. I was in the parking lot. I assumed she came back here. That's what she normally does."

He eyed her for a bit before excusing himself. She didn't know where he went, but he was gone five minutes too long. That made her suspect something was up. He also shouldn't have been hounding her like he was. If Salazar knew Jas was nice on her, Martí should've known, too. All he should've been doing was going up the steps to get her. If he was, Carmen couldn't tell. Whatever he was doing was eating up time. Still, Carmen remained in the foyer. She thought about going upstairs to Dumati's room, but she couldn't do it unprotected. She also couldn't do it without Kane. Therefore, she stayed where she was.

Footsteps approached, leading her to turn towards the sound. Before her eyes could focus on who was beside her, the person knocked her unconscious. When she did wake, she didn't know how long she'd been out. There wasn't a clock in the bedroom, and she couldn't see outside the window. What she did know was that she had a pounding headache. In addition, there was a gun pointed at her. Martí was sitting in a chair, a gun in one hand, a phone in the other. He raised the phone to his ear.

"If you're looking for your bitch, I have her."

Those words told her he was talking to Kane.

"Your bitch ain't your bitch, though," he continued. "I bet you didn't know that."

It was obvious Jas ratted her out. If Martí did his research, Kane's cover was blown, too. She didn't have a lot of pictures on the internet with him because of his job at the Triad, but there was at least two to three.

"Your bitch is married," Martí dispelled. "Married to a fuckin' Santiago. Let me handle her for ya." Seconds of silence passed. "If that's your wish, I'll respect it. I'll let you in the gate." He hung up the phone. Martí turned his attention back to her. "You were on a roll. You had Kong fooled. Had me and Salazar fooled. Shit, Jas was up your whole ass."

He didn't stop there. "I've heard of the Santiagos. Never kept up with 'em. I see Jay married a black bitch like his daddy. Does he know you're slinging your pussy all over Vegas?" Martí set his gun down. "You ain't gotta answer. I know he doesn't. If he did, he would've slit your throat. You know that's what Kong is coming to do."

Carmen didn't say anything. If anyone was getting their throat slit, it was him. Martí didn't know it, but he signed his own death certificate.

"You thought you were gonna finish what Santiago started, eh? You were tryin' to get to Ishmael. Salazar gave me permission to do you in, but I wanna watch. It's gotta be an art to kill the woman you love. Like how is Kong gonna do it? Is he gonna fuck you first?" Martí neared his face to hers. "If I was him, I would take one last dip in ya pussy." He stood up. "It doesn't matter what he does. You and Jay will end up where I want ya—in the same casket."

None of what he said fazed her. Carmen knew what was coming. All she had to do was wait it out. Little did Martí know, he was closer to a casket than she would ever be.

Sixteen

Martí's phone call sent the clock ticking. The raid was scheduled for 0600, but with Carmen held hostage in Salazar's house, Kane pre-gamed. It was never his intention for the Triad to know she was in Vegas. If they did, his contract would be up in the air like it was years ago when he fell in love with her. He had to get her out Salazar's house before they touched ground. That meant enlisting his crew to go to war with him. They were already in one of his garages helping him prepare for the raid. Three were at the front of the Escalade, removing the bumper. Three were at the back, detaching the cargo liners and seats while he and Felix took apart the dashboard.

Once they were done, the Escalade looked like bones. Machine guns, rifles, silencers, pistols, magazines, clips, and anything else that could take down an army was lined up on the garage floor. All of it had been hidden inside the Escalade. It was the reason he couldn't leave the car in Kingston. The only thing he didn't have in plentiful supply was bulletproof vests. Those went to Chico and Lomax, who were less skilled shooters. Kane knew from his visits to Salazar's house, there were at least eight men keeping guard. If Martí wasn't in the room with Carmen, he was on the ground along with three others. Four were guaranteed to be on the roof. "We gotta take out the guys up top first. Shoot to kill. Aim for the head," he instructed. "Get them before they get you."

He told them they weren't hitting the home from the front. "That's what they're expecting. We gotta hit 'em from the back." It was followed by a simple reminder. "Once that first bullet goes, we become the target. Keep shooting until everything moving is dead." Kane knew what Martí was betting on. Martí thought he bought his story and would come through the gate. That plan was a trap. If Carmen's cover was blown, his was, too.

Kane didn't share those thoughts as they loaded up one of the Triad's vans. As he did before any operation, he recited the 23rd Psalm until he was parked two blocks away from Salazar's mansion. With no time to waste, they disbanded, separating into pairs. Each group headed to a different spot on the property. Gustavo was a few strides behind him until Kane's pace decreased to a slow crept. The street they walked down brought them up on the back end of Salazar's Caribbean-modeled pool. An iron fence served as their only divider. Kane knelt in front of it although it couldn't protect him from death or from being seen.

Two armed men were on the roof, patrolling the estate. Kane made a clicking sound towards Gustavo. When he looked at him, Kane nodded towards the men. Before he could face them, the first shot rung through the air.

It's on.

The gunshots became repetitive. Kane didn't wait for Salazar's muscle to move. He pointed and fired, the first bullet grazing one of the men's cheeks. The pain sent the man firing at anything he could. Bullet after bullet whizzed past Kane's head until he fired a fatal shot that blew off the man's nose. When his body dropped, so did his partner's. Gustavo had taken him out.

The Lord is my shepherd.

That didn't mean they were finished. That meant war had started. Both gunfire and death were in the air. Men came running from different corners of the property. Their presence called for a change in the recipe. With a machine gun now in his hands, Kane splattered them one by one until the only thing moving was a body falling dead in the pool. "Move," he yelled. They ran around the back of the property, gunfire still erupting. When it ceased, Kane slowed his pace, now approaching the backside of Salazar's second pool. Patheros and Felix were aimed at the roof despite the dead bodies upon it.

Kane made a whistling sound to alert them of his presence. He signaled for them to take off, making a mental note that eight men were down. He then upped his pace, passing Patheros and Felix, until more gunfire sounded. Almost at the front entrance, he tightened his grip on the trigger. He loosened it when he saw Chico and Lomax. They were standing over a body, who he noted as the ninth man. He whistled again. More gunfire sounded, sending them on the ground for cover. It came and went like gun smoke.

I shall not want.

Without the gun blasts, the sound of nighttime elevated in Kane's ears. He ignored the pulsing of his heart, concentrating on his surroundings. Faint grunting was in the distance. The sound sent Kane to his feet, the others following his lead.

He maketh me to lie down in green pastures.

What they came to find was Julio and Martí at the front entrance. Martí was riddled with bullets while Julio had taken one to the chest. Jose was putting pressure on the wound, trying to control the bleeding. Kane shielded them from what he was feeling as emotion wasn't going to keep Julio alive. Action was. He tossed his keys to Gustavo. "Get him to a hospital." He then turned towards the rest of them. "Y'all gotta go. The police can't be far away. They only need to find me."

The directive given, he raced inside the house. His machine gun went in its holster while his pistol went back in his hands. Now, in the foyer, he listened to the silence.

Salazar don't move like his son.

Although now defunct, Dumati had an army, Artemis 66. After the U.S. captured most of them and Jay eliminated a group at The Ave, it was obvious Dumati had little to no back-up. Salazar kept his circle small, which is why Kane was able to take his men down without the Triad. Judging from how calm it was, if anything was to occur at six o'clock, it was the Triad tracking every single security camera or plane for leads on where Salazar or Dumati could be.

The silence made Kane question if anyone was there. If someone was, they would've shot at him. He also wouldn't have been able to make it up the steps. Not hearing any movements, he peered down the hall. The way was clear. When he headed around the corner, an unexpected blast took him down.

He leadeth me beside the still waters.

Brick's face wore a sinister grin. "I told you I can get some work."

Kane gritted his teeth at the mounting pressure in his arm. He could smell his flesh burning. Expletives sat at the tip of his tongue. "That's the best you got?"

"Oh, I wasn't tryin' to take you down with this." Brick dropped his gun on the floor. "I'm tryin' to take you down with this." He reached in his pocket and pulled out a badge. "King muthafuckin' Kong, Britain's been waiting on you for eighteen years." He now spoke in an English accent. "What is this? Like five for the price of one? All I wanted was Presi. Oh, don't worry about your bitch. I didn't hit her too hard."

Di investigation. Make it go away.

Kane stared at the MI6 badge in Brick's hand. Presi was right. Someone was investigating him. That someone being the UK's Secret Service Intelligence Agency. He now remembered his assignment, the task he took in exchange for Salazar's name. Kane had to give it to Presi. He was smart. By giving him the task, Presi eliminated Brick and had something to hang over his head. He also did it far away from Jamaican soil.

The pick-up was never a pick-up. Or at least not on Kane's part. It was a drop-off. It was a pick-up for whoever collected Brick's remains. The money he delivered to Salazar was payment for the disposal of Brick's body. To this day, they were still waiting for it. The only reason Kane was hesitating now is because he was taken aback at how everything revealed itself. All it took was Brick flashing his badge. Now it was time for him to flash his.

"I'm Triad, you fuckin' bitch."

Brick's eyes widened. Kane let the realization sit with him before he lodged a bullet in the center of Brick's forehead. When he went down, Kane dropped his pistol. His eyes traveled to his arm only to see another body laid out in the hallway. He grabbed his pistol, attempting to stand as he stared at the woman. He could tell from her complexion she wasn't Carmen. The body shape told him she wasn't Jas. She was bleeding out, her trembles telling him if he didn't move quick, she would be another casualty.

"Carm," he yelled, making it to his feet. He held his hand over his wound, the pain growing every second. "Carm," he yelled again. He opened the door to the first room he came to. It was empty. He went to the second, the third, the fourth, the fifth, until he found her. Her hands were tied around her back while numerous gags were in her mouth. "I got you," he told her. He threw his gun on the bed, using his good hand to undo the knot around her hands. He struggled with it until footsteps forced him to drop it all together. He pointed his pistol at the doorway right when Lownes walked in. "Son of a bitch."

"Hello to you, too," Lownes replied. "Long time no see." He went straight for Carmen. He pulled the gags out her mouth. "You got a blood bath out there." He untied the bandanas around her wrists.

Kane ignored him, grabbing one of the bandanas. He tied up his arm, hoping it would stop the bleeding long enough for him to get Dumati. "Take this," he said, handing Carmen his pistol. He shot a look in Lownes' direction. "In case we get more company." He kept his eyes on him. "Did you hear police out there?"

"Your plug was trying to make a run for it," Lownes announced. He used the word plug on purpose as a hint to Kane he knew about his involvement in Salazar's operation. "He's in a stand-off with the Vegas PD and Triad at McCarran Airport. They ain't gonna be over here for a while."

Kane cursed under his breath. His eyes went to Carmen who was holding his pistol. "The lady in the hall," he began. "Can you stay with her? Try to keep her alive."

"She ain't gonna make it," Lownes told him. "She caught one in the neck."

Carmen overlooked what Lownes said. Her attention was on Kane's arm. "We need to get you to a hospital." She tried to remove the bandana to examine his wound. All Kane gave her was a stare. Twenty years of marriage taught them how to communicate without words. She read his face, which told her to do as he asked.

Carmen tended to the woman who Kane now knew was Mija. Meanwhile, he and Lownes stood on both sides of the door Carmen suspected to be Dumati's. Pistol in hand, Kane reached for the knob. He turned it while Lownes kicked it open. The aggression that was once there was replaced with fear. Kane dropped his weapon at his side.

An empty hospital bed was in the room. In front of it was a wheelchair, where one of the biggest terrorists known to man sat. A time bomb was strapped to his chest. Ten minutes was left on the clock. Or as Kane saw it, ten minutes to decide between fight or flight.

He restoreth my soul.

Dumati didn't move. He didn't even look their way. His eyes were focused on one spot on the wall. If it wasn't for him blinking, Kane would've thought he was dead. He took a step inside, studying the man's posture. His eyes then gazed over the rest of the room. When he spotted boxes of catheter tubes, his suspicions were confirmed. The man was now a paraplegic. Dumati's condition explained why he chose death. Unable to care for himself, he didn't have the means to run. He also didn't have support from his father. Salazar abandoned him, choosing to save himself.

Kane watched as Dumati's face turned towards his. The man's lips parted.

"Tell Santiago I'll see him in hell."

Kane jumped out his skin. The gunshot had come out of nowhere. He stood there, frozen, staring at the gaping hole that was now stamped in the upper left corner of Dumati's forehead.

"We ain't got time." Lownes pushed past him. He grabbed Dumati's remains, throwing him on the floor. "Snap out of it, Kane. This thing is still going."

Kane looked behind him to see Carmen in the hallway. Her grip was firm on the pistol, the barrel still pointed in the direction of Dumati's chair.

"Wake the fuck up," Lownes yelled at him. "We got eight fuckin' minutes."

Kane came back to reality. He dropped to the floor, watching as the seconds changed on the clock. "I would let his ass burn if this body weren't our fuckin' payday. He blows up, this whole operation is a bust." He unstrapped the bomb from Dumati's chest, turning it over to see the wires. There was a total of six at the bottom, two red, two blue, one yellow, and one black. There were also five buttons with various symbols and letters. "I never saw the back of one of his bombs. This is some new shit."

Lownes agreed. "I only saw the remains of 'em."

Kane glanced at Lownes when the timer went to seven. "Let's grab Dumati and let the house go down. We got seven minutes flat."

"What do you have to make charges stick on Salazar?"

"Some of his finest coke," Kane replied. "No telling what's in this house, though. It could be a mistake to let it go down." His eyes went to the bomb until a shadow appeared. Too big to be Carmen, he looked over his shoulder to see Jay's right-hand. "You gotta be fuckin' kiddin' me."

"You have to disarm each module," Cesar told him.

Kane looked at Carmen who was closing Mija's eyes. He turned back to Cesar. "What are you doing here?"

Cesar gave him four words. "Buying my ticket home." He was on the Triad's Most Wanted list for his role in a shootout that occurred at Jay's restaurant, Blue Magic. If it wasn't for Jay faking his death, Cesar would've been prosecuted with him. The Triad discovered he was alive when they saw the security footage from The Ave. It showed him taking out Dumati's men.

Cesar knelt between Kane and Lownes. He pulled a pair of pliers out his jacket before grabbing the bomb. He pointed at the first button. "A star has five points. We clip the fifth wire."

"Whoa," Kane said, grabbing Cesar's hand. "You can't just go clippin' shit."

Cesar's words were sharp. "I clip this, or you spend the last five minutes of your life trying to get out."

They stared each other down until Kane gave him a head nod. As much as he didn't want to put his life in Cesar's hands, he was the one who diffused the bomb at The Ave. It still went off, but not at the magnitude it should have.

Cesar clipped the yellow wire. "The second button is a triangle. Three points." He clipped the third wire, a red one. He then moved to the third button, which was labeled with the paragraph marks symbol.

"There's no points on that," Lownes noticed.

"We're at four minutes," Kane stressed. He looked behind him to see Carmen crying. "Get out of here," he yelled. "Don't wait for me. Go."

"The black fill," he heard Cesar say. "It could represent the black wire."

Kane watched as Carmen stood up. She mouthed I love you. He mouthed it back as Cesar clipped the black wire. When she ran towards the stairwell, his attention went back to the bomb.

"The letter B," Cesar was saying.

"It could be for blue," Kane suggested. "There's two modules labeled B, one uppercase, one lowercase." He stared at the buttons then at the wires. "The loops," he told him. "The uppercase B has two loops. The lowercase B has one loop. Clip the blue wires, those wires are the first and second in the line-up. It matches the loops."

"What's up with this Riddler shit? This ain't fuckin' *Batman*," Lownes barked.

"It is if you think like a maniac," Cesar retorted. "In his fucked up mind," he said, speaking of Dumati, "he may think he's giving you a chance to live."

"What went wrong at the Ave?" Kane asked. "Why did that one go off?"

Cesar clipped the second wire, a blue one. "It was my first time seeing one of his bombs. There was only one module, a puzzle piece. There were ten wires. I used luck to disarm it."

He leadeth me in the paths of righteousness for His name's sake.

Three minutes was left on the clock. Kane watched as Cesar got ready to clip the last blue wire. He grabbed his hand to stop him. "What if the lowercase B stands for blood? Blood is red." He looked at Dumati to see a pool of blood forming underneath his head.

"That's logical," Cesar replied. "It could be either one. If this bomb is like the one at The Ave, if we clip the wrong one, the timer will keep going. If it's the right one, the timer will stop. It could be blue. Or it could be red. It's something we gotta decide together."

Lownes was pacing the floor. "This ain't no flip a quarter type shit." His words referenced *Batman* again; however, this time, it was the character Two-Face.

Yea, though I walk through the valley of the shadow of death, I will fear no evil.

"Clip the red wire," Kane said, thinking of the red diamonds. Out of all the things Dumati could have shipped to Vegas, he chose three small stones. "It's that one."

Cesar hesitated. "If it's the wrong one, we got less than two minutes to get out of here."

For thou art with me. Thy rod and thy staff they comfort me.

Lownes spoke up. "You said the timer will keep going. If it does, we'll clip the blue one."

"The bomb will still go off because we clipped the wrong one," Kane explained. "There's a possibility it won't be as bad, but we don't have time for possibilities. If Dumati was set on dying, this whole house is coming down." He stared at the pliers in Cesar's hands. "It's the red one. I swear on my kids' lives. If you clip the blue one, we're dead. If you clip the red one, you won't die with your best friend's enemy."

Cesar gave him a death stare. "Jay's only enemy is himself."

Those words meant nothing to Kane. He didn't care about Jay's demons. What he cared about was seeing his children graduate college, become wives, husbands, mothers, and fathers. "Leviticus 17:11," Kane told them. "For the life of the flesh is in the blood." He stood on his feet as the clock went to one minute. "Blood is red. Clip it." He walked towards the window. Tears returned to his eyes. "Thou preparest a table before me in the presence of mine enemies. Thou anointest my head with oil; my cup runneth over. Surely goodness and mercy shall follow me all the days of my life." He heard Cesar as he clipped the wire. "And I will dwell in the house of the Lord forever."

Cesar let out a large breath. "It stopped."

Kane lowered himself to his knees. Inaudible words flowed out his mouth as he prayed for minutes on end. When he concluded his prayer, Lownes and Cesar were carrying Dumati's remains down the steps. With his arm out of commission, he couldn't lift Brick or Mija. What he could do was place a call to King. Brick's death needed to stay under the radar, which meant his body couldn't go to the hospital. If anyone knew how to hide a body, it was King. He watched Jay hide a few of them. It took longer than he wanted, but he got it. Ten minutes later, Brick's remains were loaded inside a van belonging to Mendez Funeral Home.

Once the van was out of sight, the sirens came.

SEVENTEEN

The blood bath Kane caused at Salazar's mansion was miniscule compared to what occurred at McCarran Airport. Salazar was set on leaving the city and brought enough firepower to make it happen. Or so he thought. The death toll was so large, the Triad and Vegas PD said little about the twelve deaths that occurred on Kane's watch. After little to no questioning, Kane was transported to the hospital. Agents surrounded him, making it impossible for him to call Carmen with his whereabouts. She also couldn't be present when a bullet was removed from his arm.

Unlike a slew of other agents, he walked out the hospital with only a sling. Kane returned home to find Carmen waiting for him in the living room. They didn't say much, their body language speaking for them. The moment he sat on the couch; she was in his arms. He held her to his chest as they both fell asleep.

The following morning, they sat across from each other, making decisions about the house and cars. The Jaguar, which Kane admitted to buying, would be transported to New York along with Carmen's Benz. The mansion would become a rental property to help Carmen recoup some of the millions she spent.

With a plan finalized, Kane met up with Felix and Gustavo while Carmen packed up the house. Their first stop was Mendez Funeral Home. Upon arriving, two undertakers placed Brick's bagged remains in the back of the Triad van. Fifteen minutes later, Felix and Gustavo placed the deceased inside a Sysco truck parked behind La Gran Carnicería. Although Salazar was now in federal custody, Kane completed the assignment for Presi.

After thanking Felix and Gustavo for their time and service, he returned home. Carmen had purchased two one-way flights to Brookstone and was hard at work on packing. Kane helped her where he could until it was done. Both worn out, they went their separate ways. She retired inside the master bedroom while he took one of the remaining four.

For Carmen, sleep was a stranger. Her body was tired, but her mind was wide awake. Her mind was in a battle between good and evil. While Kane was out, she called Jay to update him on what occurred. The conversation didn't start off pleasant as he was bothered by the way she left and her lack of communication. She was able to get his mood to change when she told him she killed Dumati. That got him promising to outfit her in a twelve million dollar necklace and another good dickdown. With her husband on her conscience, she struggled to fight her urges.

Her body hungered for Kane. If there was ever a perfect time for sex, it was the night before. After they took down Salazar and Dumati, she should've rocked his world. Instead of laying in post-coital bliss, they laid fully clothed in each other's arms. It was fine for the moment, but now, she needed more. It wasn't horniness like it had been some other times they sexed. It was love.

Carmen needed Kane to feed her one more time before they stopped for good. However, the guilt she had from the desire wouldn't allow her to tell him. She fought the urge every second, every minute, every hour. She even watched their sex tape to cope. That sent her into an orgasmic spell without her even touching herself. It got her to sleep, but she didn't stay there. She saw Kane in her dreams. It didn't matter where she was. If she was at Flame, she saw him on an elevator. If she was in the home gym, he came knocking on the door. Everywhere she turned, he was there. Then, she decided not to fight it. She climbed out of bed and opened the door.

The feeling was mutual. Carmen closed the door behind her and sat in front of it. Across the hall, Kane sat in front of his. They stared at each other, neither of them talking or moving. They were both trying to fight what their bodies desired.

The worst part was that Kane had nothing to lose. She had Jay. Her husband didn't deserve any of the sinful things she did. For weeks, he fought for his life, after saving hers. If he hadn't of pushed her out harm's way, Dumati's bullets would've gotten her, too. In return, she gave him infidelity, betrayal, and heartbreak, the worst three-course meal served on a platter.

She promised her father she would take care of him. She promised Jay she would be a good wife. She couldn't do that if she allowed Kane to penetrate her again. It would only continue her descent into the rabbit hole. Although it pained her to do it, Carmen changed her mind. She got up, went back in the room, and locked the door. Fresh tears brought sleep her way.

***

Two Weeks Later

The engine was so loud, Carmen thought Gully parked the limo in her foyer. As if that wasn't enough, his voice was booming on the other side of Jay's bedroom door.

"Tell Boss Man to act like he wants to run again. We 'bout to be late."

"You hear that?" Carmen laughed while Jay rolled his eyes. "Your cousin is a trip."

Jay was quick with a response. "He wouldn't be doing all that if he knew what physical therapy does to me. That shit hurts. That's why I ain't in a rush."

"You're making progress, though," Carmen voiced. "You're not using your chair as much. I see you more on the walker than anything."

"That ain't from physical therapy," Jay countered. He grabbed the walker, leaning his weight on it. "That's from you riding this dick every night."

"I don't wanna hear that shit," Gully shouted. "Bring yo ass on."

Carmen busted out laughing. "He heard you." She grabbed Jay's face and gave him a huge kiss. "I'll check in with you in an hour or so. I gotta get Bella together. You know she's going back with Kane."

For the past two weeks, Bella had been living with her while Kane recovered from his gunshot wound. He still wasn't fully healed, but her ex felt he was strong enough to care for her. The first night Bella was at her house, Carmen questioned if Jay even looked at her. When the third night rolled around, she left Bella alone with him while she pretended to go upstairs. It took about ten minutes, but eventually he picked her up. She then heard his cries.

"Why couldn't you be mine?" he cried. "I wanted another little girl." Bella cooed in response. "I wanted her to look like you."

Those words brought tears to Carmen's eyes. From that moment on, Jay treated Bella like she was his own. It got awkward when Kane stopped by for visits, but Jay handled the situation maturely. In Carmen's opinion, everything was looking up. There were good vibes in the house, her marriage was strong, and she was even going to therapy. The only thing she had to straighten out was Flame. Before that could happen, though, she had to hand Bella over.

"See, she's all ready for you," Carmen told Kane as she put Bella in his arms. "Look at that smile. She didn't even do all that for me."

"Don't be jealous," Kane joked. He rocked Bella in his arms before placing a kiss on the baby's cheeks. "I heard the limo when I was pulling up. I guess Jay is on his way out."

"He is," Carmen replied. "They're probably pulling off now. He has physical therapy."

Kane placed Bella in her car seat. "I've been so busy, you know, wrapping up the case and all, we haven't gotten the chance to talk."

Carmen braced herself.

"I can see that you're happy," he continued. "I'm not gonna mess with that. I've accepted that we're over. I know we're not gonna be together. I do feel like I need to address some things, though. The tape we made. No one will see that. All those sex-filled days and nights, going to a grave. I'll never tell anyone what we did. I talked to God and repented."

Kane let out a short chuckle. "You didn't want to hear all that. I just felt I needed to say it."

Carmen blushed. "I appreciate it. I know these past two weeks have been hard."

Kane chuckled again. "It has been. Our tape gets me through those cold nights, though."

Carmen covered her face. "Well," she stressed, bringing her hands back down. "I'm glad. May the memory live on."

"You know you rode the hell out me, right?"

Carmen put her hands up. "Stop, we ain't goin' no further," she said with a laugh.

"My bad." Kane picked up Bella's bags. "I better stop while I'm ahead."

"Just so you know," Carmen told him. "I'm resigning today from Flame. I'm still going to stay on as a consultant of sorts, but Jerry will be President."

"I never thought this day would come."

Carmen could agree there. "If you asked me a year ago, I would've said never. Right now, all I want to do is be a wife and mom. Rakim is going to kindergarten in September. We put him in this new Pre-K program to prepare him. He's super smart, but he needs to be around more kids. Jay and I are still searching for the perfect Pre-K program for Nyla."

"Have you—" Kane began, but Carmen cut him off.

"Don't," she urged. He was about to bring up Tiara. Her best friend since she was in middle school, the two had a major falling out almost two months ago when Carmen learned she was responsible for putting out her sex tapes. Tiara took it a step further when she invited Dumati to her party at The

Ave. In her friend's defense, she didn't know it was him as Dumati was using a fake name, but she still had done it.

Kane dismissed the conversation. "No need to go there. I guess I'll leave on that note." He gave Carmen a quick peck on the cheek before leaving the house.

Carmen left shortly after. Linx drove her to Flame where she spent the day tying up loose ends, reviewing press releases, and putting out fires. When five-thirty rolled around, she called Linx to pick her up. When she didn't get him, she texted. After ten minutes went by without a response, she called Roman. She got his voicemail, which led her to call Gully. He answered on the third ring.

Carmen heard a lot of noise in the background. "Where are y'all?" she asked. "This is the first time I've called for a ride and no one's answering."

Gully barked his words, "What do you want?"

"What's with the attitude?" she shot back. "I just told you what I wanted. Did something happen today?" She didn't give him a chance to answer. "I need someone to pick me up."

"Call your husband," Gully replied.

"About what? Because I need a ride? Why? We do this every day, all day."

Gully's tone didn't change. "No one is coming. Call an Uber and call your husband."

The phone hung up in her face.

EIGHTEEN

Carmen followed Gully's advice. She called an Uber and she called Jay. She didn't get him, catching his voicemail twice, which led her to send a text. By the time she got home, he hadn't returned her call. At that point, she didn't need him to. Fiona was in the foyer in hysterics while Kristian and Akaila were trying to console and question her all at the same time.

"Can someone please tell me what's going on?" Carmen screamed.

Fiona wasn't good for anyone. She was crying and hollering in both English and Spanish.

"She's been like this since we got here," Kristian explained.

Carmen shook her head in disbelief. Unsure of what to do, she opened the door to Jay's room. At the sight of it, she gasped. Aside from the furniture, the room was empty. *Something is wrong.* She didn't say anything to Fiona or her daughters, taking off up the steps. She headed to her bedroom as it was the closest room to the stairwell. Everything was in its proper place until she got to her closet. Every single item of Jay's was gone. *What is going on?* She ran out the room and down the hall. She opened the door to Rakim's room and dropped to her knees. Her son's toys, books, games, all of it was gone. The door to his closet was open, allowing her to see that Jay had taken his clothes, too.

What the fuck is going on?

She didn't bother to check Nyla's room. She already knew what to expect. What she did was call Jay. He didn't answer. She called him again. He didn't answer. She called him again, again, again, and again, until he picked up. When he did, he unleashed venom.

"You tired of fuckin'?" His volume scared her more than his words. "Yeah, yeah, I heard you. I heard y'all asses. Day and night? Oh, his ass got it like that. You slut ass bitch. I bet you thought you were good. You thought you'd gotten away with it. Y'all muthafuckas slipped. I heard y'all. Don't lie. I heard you. I was takin' a fuckin' shit. Came out the bathroom and heard y'all asses. You fucked him? You fucked him? You fuckin' no good black bitch. You're just like your fuckin' mama. The apple doesn't fall far from the fuckin' tree. She raised you well. Made you a fuckin' build-a-whore bitch. Fuck you, Carmen. Fuck you. I'll fuckin' slit your throat."

Once again, Carmen dropped to the floor.

"I fuckin' hate you," he yelled. "You did this shit. You see what you did? Look at what you did to me. Look at what you did to us. Why, Carmen? Why?" The tears were coming. "Why did you do this? The garage? Is that when it started? Were you fuckin' him then? Gully thought you were. Cesar told me not to jump to conclusions. When you came home and was ridin' me. I felt it. That's why I stopped you. You learned that from him. You fucked him and brought your dirty pussy home to me. I've been eatin' you out every fuckin' day. I've been lickin' your fuckin' shit. You knew he had cum in you. You had me lickin' his shit. Then, he said y'all taped it. You dirty ass bitch. Wait till I get my hands on you. I'm fuckin' up your shit."

Carmen couldn't speak. She could barely think.

"You had him livin' in our house." Jay was still going. "I understood when Gully explained it. His wife died. I got it. Now I see it was just quick access for y'all to fuck. I bet you did him in my bed. You nasty bitch." The tears were disappearing, his volume escalating to an even higher level. "I was fightin' for my fuckin' life. I was fightin' for my fuckin' life, Carm. Why were you fuckin' him?"

Jay didn't give her a chance to speak. He kept going. Carmen let him, too. In the middle of his curses, screams, and threats, she packed a bag. She grabbed her laptop and bought a one way ticket to San Juan. She knew that was where he was. There was no way he, the kids, Silvas, and his right-hands were piled in his penthouse apartment where Gully lived.

Carmen let him unleash his anger. She deserved it. She was wrong and it was time for her to pay. She let him rage until she couldn't any longer. When she walked in the airport, she hung up the phone. She didn't put her phone back to her ear until she was outside the gate of their San Juan estate. "Silvas," she said, trying for a third time to input the gate code. She called Jay's butler because she knew he would help her. "Jay changed the code. I'm trying to get inside. I need to talk to him."

"I can't let you in," Silvas told her. "It's not safe."

"I know he's upset," Carmen cried. "I know I fucked up." She struggled to speak. "I need to talk to him. I need him to know I'm sorry. All that is over. I need him to know."

Silvas spoke, calmly. "Carmen Denise Santiago, I need you to hear me clearly. Jay is in the middle of an episode. It's not safe. It's not safe for anyone. Gully and Linx bound him to his bed. We put the kids in another wing of the house so they can't hear him. I need you to leave."

Carmen swallowed at his words. "Y'all tied him to a bed? Why? When? How?" Shock overcame her. "Look, I need to get my kids. They need to be with me."

"You can't get them. Go home. Let Jay get through this."

Those were Silvas' last words before he disconnected the call. Carmen didn't know what to do or where to turn. She wanted to see Jay. She needed to explain. He needed to hear her apology. She wanted to tell him she was wrong. She needed him to understand the affair was over.

Y'all bound him to a fuckin' bed. That part disturbed her. *What was he trying to do?*

Carmen stared at their home. On the outside, all she saw was architectural beauty. The inside told a different story. While she wanted to hop the fence to get inside, she didn't have the physical means to do so. Therefore, she called for a taxi. She told the driver to take her to the DoubleTree Hotel where she got a room for two nights. Once she was settled, she dialed Kane's number only for Jay to beep in. *He can't be tied up if he's calling me. Maybe he's calmed down.*

She answered her phone.

"Why did you do it?" was the first thing out Jay's mouth. He was much calmer than before. Although he posed the question, he didn't give her a chance to respond. "I'm not dumb, Carm. I know you love him. Like, you gotta love him to stay married to him for twenty years. I know those feelings don't go away. You said you loved me, though. You married me. Don't chu feel something for me, too?" He then spoke as if he was trying to convince himself of the truth. "You love me. I know you love me. The way you look at me. You gotta love me. You carried three babies for me."

Carmen parted her lips to respond, but he kept talking.

"I called him. I told him to be a man. He fucked my wife. He can be a man and tell me. He said he fucked you. He said y'all messed around in the garage. He said y'all would've fucked, but your period was on. What the fuck, Carm? You were out there like that. You were that horny?"

The skeletons were flying out Carmen's closet.

"Why couldn't you wait for me? Why did you need it that bad? Kane told me everything. He told me what you did to him. This muthafucka told me you sucked his shit from the back. You did that shit? I've been kissing you. You did that shit and let me kiss you?" His anger switched to something else. "He said in Vegas you were his wife. You fucked him so good he thought that? I told him he should've bought your dirty ass a fuckin' ring. If you're his wife, he should've bought you a ring. You know what this muthafucka told me. He said he didn't have a ring when he first proposed. What the fuck? I gave you three fuckin' rings. I got on my knees three fuckin' times. I spent millions on your triflin' ass. But he didn't need a ring?"

He didn't stop to catch a breath. "He said you gave it to him, Carm. He said you gave him my diamond. He said you put the Pink Sunrise in his fuckin' wedding band. You did that shit? You gave him my fuckin' shit? You stole my shit and gave it to him. Run, bitch. Bitch, you better run. I swear, I'm slicin' your shit from ear to ear."

Jay was speaking of a lie she told Kane years ago. She did tell him she put the Pink Sunrise in his wedding band. The truth of the matter was that she didn't. It was a mind game. She only told him that to prove how easily he could've gotten the location of the diamond if he asked. Since there was a pink diamond in his wedding band, Kane wouldn't have known if it was the truth or not. Now ready to reveal her secret, she couldn't as Jay didn't let her get a word in.

"Is that why you couldn't turn it in?" Jay continued. "Is that why you gave the government a fake?" He brought up the deal he made with Uncle Sam. After seventeen years in prison, in exchange for his freedom, he agreed to turn in the Pink Sunrise. The problem was, he didn't have it. During the Blue Magic trial, the powers that be were set on locking him up for life. Jay hadn't made good on his promise, and they were growing impatient. When Gomez delivered the news to her that Jay was facing life, she aligned herself with a jeweler and a chemist. A replica of the Pink Sunrise was created. When tested, it would appear to be real. By the time anyone learned it wasn't, she and Jay would be dead and gone.

"It's him," Jay was now saying. "You ain't out here just fuckin', you're fuckin' him. You want him. You'll tear me down to get him, too. You'll make sure I suffer if it means you can have him."

He was silent for a split second, which allowed Carmen to get a word in. "We both know I fucked up. When I came home from Vegas, I told you I needed to work on me. I told you I was gonna go to therapy. I knew something was wrong. There had to be for me to let something like that happen. I needed to process my feelings."

Carmen paused only briefly. "You want full transparency; I'll give it to you. Yes, I love him. I love the hell out of him. I'll go deeper and admit I'm in love with him. I didn't know it when we first messed around. I did that on some payback shit for Monifah. That was when we thought she was the one who put out my sex tapes. But when I did it, I realized how deep my feelings were. Our marriage was so dark at the time," she said speaking of her and Jay. "We had so many issues. I didn't have that with him. Kane and I were like each other's escape. Still, I wasn't leaving you. I also knew he wasn't leaving Monifah. That's one thing we both stood on. Even when we were in Vegas, Kane knew I wasn't leaving you for him. I'm your wife 'til my last breath."

Carmen swallowed. "I love you to my core. I know my actions didn't show it, but I do. I'm obsessed with you. Addicted. You make me mad, we break up, but I come right back every single time. It's because I can't live without you. I need you to breathe." She wiped her tears. "You may not see it now, but we're gonna get through this. Just like we've gotten through other shit." Her tears continued to come. "What me and Kane did was wrong. We know it. If you heard us, you heard us say it was over. We're not messing around. I promise. I swear, Jay, we didn't do this to hurt you. We were selfish and we got caught up."

"Fuck you," Jay roared. "You did it to hurt me. Every time you opened your legs and let him cum inside you, you hurt me. You're my fuckin' wife. You're not gonna do me like him, Carm. You're not gonna fuckin' do me like him. You were fuckin' me when you were with him. Remember? You're not gonna do that to me. You're not gonna fuck around on me. You hear me? Did you get that? I want a divorce. I want a fuckin' divorce. I don't want you. You can die and go to hell. I'll send you. I'll cut your fuckin' heart out. I'll bite your fuckin'—"

Carmen heard tussling and then the phone fell silent. She didn't know who took the phone from him, but she was certain because of his threats he wouldn't get it back. He did, though. He called later that night. She asked to speak to the kids. He ignored her, choosing to call her a bitch, whore, devil, and threaten her life for a full ten minutes before she hung up. He didn't call back until the following morning. After being denied access to the kids again, he ranted for two minutes before she hung up on him a second time.

Still, she answered when he called back that night. This time, he wasn't speaking. He was masturbating. Never in her twenty-two years of knowing him had she ever seen or heard him stroke his dick. Since he called her, she figured he was fantasizing about her. Perhaps, it was a sign he was coming around. He was loud with it, too. Not his moans per se, but whatever he was doing to himself, she heard it through the phone. He didn't speak to her, keeping at it until he came. Then, the phone hung up.

The next day, Carmen didn't answer when he called. She was busy checking out the hotel. She then boarded a flight back to Brookstone. When she landed, she called Kristian to pick her up. Right when her daughter pulled up, she received a call from Gomez. Jay threatened divorce twenty times, so she took the call.

"I'm not even going to drag this out," Gomez began. "Jay asked me to start a divorce petition. I laughed at him. I told him I don't do family law. I'm criminal." Gomez chuckled for a bit. "Look, Carm, he told me what happened. He wants to divorce you. I told him not to, for this sole reason here. He loves the hell out of you. This dude cried in my face for seventeen years over you. Look, I understand his anger, his frustration. I get it. I probably shouldn't say this because I practice law, but I want to whoop your ass. At the same time, I don't recommend divorce. I told him it's a waste of money. He's mad, and he should be, but he needs to calm down before filing a petition. The wound is fresh. I'm tryin' to talk him into just separating. I told him to stay in San Juan."

"A filing is a filing," Carmen told him. "It ain't a divorce." She got inside Kristian's car. "Let him waste his money." She listened to Gomez for a few more minutes before the call ended. By the time she got home, Jay had called her twice. She didn't answer. She focused on Akaila and Kristian who had been home by themselves for the past couple of days. At first she didn't think it was a big deal until she realized there was no security at the estate. There also weren't any men on the property. She called Malachi and asked him to move back in. He told he her couldn't, reminding her about the three-day field trip he had with his Science class. He then told her he didn't want to. He wanted no parts of the drama.

That prompted her to call King. Her son told her off, telling her Jay had told him everything. King even reminded her that he asked about her and Kane's relationship a while ago. "I ain't gettin' in y'alls shit. You've been going back and forth between them before I was born. You deal with that. I got my own family to look after. Keep your legs closed."

Carmen retired to her room and called Cesar. She didn't get him, but his wife answered. She kindly let her know that Cesar wouldn't be taking her calls. She was nice about it, told Carmen she was praying for her then hung up the phone. Minutes later, another call from Jay came through. Carmen ignored him. She didn't want to hear what a horrible person she was. She knew it. She felt it. Still, Jay kept calling. She let him get her voicemail.

Concerned about the estate's security, Carmen went to sleep with an idea in mind. It was the worst thing she could come up with, but it was her only option. She got the reminder when she was woken out her sleep. Her bedroom door hit the wall, sending her eyes open.

Gully was standing in her doorway.

"Are you fuckin' crazy?" she yelled at him. She glanced at her alarm clock. "It's three in the morning."

"Yeah, I'm crazy, and your bipolar ass husband is, too," Gully shouted. He slammed her door closed. "Why weren't you answering your phone?"

"You didn't hear him?" she bellowed. "How many bitches am I gonna be?"

"You're a fuckin' dumb ass," Gully roared. "You should appreciate a good cussin' out. He could be goin' upside ur damn head. Shit. He's callin' night and day to make sure yo ass is safe. You weren't answering so he made me and Roman fly over here to see about your cheatin' ass."

"Tell him to let y'all stay and he won't have to call."

"Fuck you, Carm," Gully spat. "No one wants to be around you. You were fuckin' around with Kane right under our noses. You better be glad Jay had enough sense to get out this house. At least he got that part right. If he had seen you, he would've killed you. Now can we get him to wash his ass? He too big to be sitting up there stinkin'. Silvas can barely walk up the steps and gotta go in there and wash his big ass. We can't even let the kids see him. Do you know what this is doing to them? They can't see their mama or their daddy." Gully wiped the sweat from his face. "Let Jay cuss ya. It's better than him breakin' your fuckin' jaw. Shit, I want to slap your ass."

Carmen jerked the covers off. "Come on, then," she told him. "Come on. I'll fuck up a dude. Ask your cousin. He'll tell you."

"I ain't puttin' my hands on you," Gully muttered. He opened her door. "Answer your phone when he calls. Tired of dealin' with y'all shit. Your pussy can't be that good."

Carmen gave him the finger. When he left the room, she got back in bed, but she couldn't sleep. She was too angry. Eventually, she did, only to be awakened by Jay when he called. She answered like Gully advised. Before he could get good and going, she told him her thoughts. "I need you to let Roman stay. There isn't any security here. I tried calling Cesar to see if we can get somebody, but he's not taking my calls. I'm suggesting Roman because he's dating Akaila. You didn't take him from me, you took him from her."

"I ain't doing shit," was Jay's response.

"You're forcin' my hand."

"What does that mean?" Jay asked.

"We need a man in the house. No one is available but Kane. He's the only option I have."

"Burn in hell." He dropped the call.

The next morning, when Jay called, she asked him again to let Roman come home. At that point, he and Gully had flown back to San Juan. Jay responded with another rant except this one he did in Spanish. She hung up after two minutes. If the calls were like Gully said, to make sure she was safe, she didn't need to spend fifteen minutes getting cussed out. One or two minutes could suffice.

With Jay refusing to help her, Carmen went to Plan B. She called Kane. He apologized to her, but she didn't care to hear it. It was best for all parties if every skeleton was on the table.

She asked him to move in. "I know it's dangerous," she said, "but I can't get through to Jay. We need someone here. It's just me and the girls."

"I'll come," Kane told her. "I'll pack up me and Bella's things. It's not a problem."

Kane kept his word and when Jay called her that night, Carmen told him what she did. He overlooked it. His voice was much calmer, but it had been that way on one of their previous calls. It's like things would start out good, a switch would be flipped, then he would turn into a raging lion.

"I dreamt about us last night," he told her. "We were here in my room. We were in bed." Carmen didn't know where the story was going, but she listened. "We were fuckin' up some sheets," he said with a chuckle. "We always fuck up some sheets. You were screaming. You know I love when you scream." He chuckled some more. "I was fuckin' the hell out yo ass. I was tearin' your pussy up. Then, I came, Peaches. The shit hit me so hard. I couldn't take it. The nut was so strong. It did something to me. Before I knew it, I was choking you. You couldn't breathe. You…"

It sounded like the phone flew across the room. Then, Silvas' voice came on the line. "Stop it. Stop it now." She heard something that sounded like a slap. "Stop this now." She heard a door slam. Seconds later, Silvas addressed her. "Do you hear how sick he is? Can you see what you did to him? I pray for you. I pray for your soul. God show mercy on your soul. I can't let you hurt him. Do you hear me? You won't hurt my son. You won't. Don't talk to him."

"I'm sorry," Carmen cried. "I am."

"Don't talk to him," Silvas replied. "Talk to me. Matter of fact, call me in the morning."

After Carmen told him she would, he disconnected the call.

NINETEEN

The first thing Carmen did when she woke was call Silvas. He didn't greet her but told her to hang up and FaceTime. She followed his directive and when he answered the video call, Rakim and Nyla were on her screen. Typically, she would hide her emotions. This time, she couldn't. She cried for minutes on end, apologizing to them, and letting them know she loved them. For the first time, she could tell they weren't happy. They were sad and confused. While Silvas and Jay's right-hands weren't strangers to them, they were rarely around the men without a parent.

"I'm gonna call y'all every day," she told them. "I love you."

Their spirit seemed to brighten, but it wasn't enough. She needed more. "I need to get them," she told Silvas. "This shit is fuckin with my babies. I can't have that. I gotta come get 'em."

"I can't take the kids out the house," Silvas replied. "If I do, we'll have to bind Jay to the bed. We had to do it last night. He went off when I took the phone. Gully and Linx could barely hold him. He won't take his pills. I called his therapist. Dr. Stuart suggested you put him on a 5150 hold. She said he needs to be stabilized."

"I can't." Carmen dismissed the idea. "They did that to him in prison. Jay and I talked about it. That's the one thing he doesn't want. If he's not being aggressive to the kids, he's good. Gully and Linx are strong. I prefer they bind him than send him to a hospital. No hold."

"Then we wait for the episode to pass."

Silvas didn't call her anymore that day, but Carmen received calls from two individuals she didn't expect to speak to. The first was from Jas. The girl had been calling her burner phone for weeks, but Carmen ignored her messages. After Jas ratted her out to Salazar and Martí, she washed her hands of her. She knew Jas was arrested at McCarran Airport, but she didn't keep up with her charges or case. The only reason Carmen accepted the call is because Jas called her personal cell. She never gave her the number, which meant Jas went through great lengths to find her.

She was still locked up, which meant Carmen had to be careful about what she said. "How did you get my number?" was the first thing out her mouth.

"The receptionist at your corporate office," Jas told her. "Why were you ignoring me?"

"You know why," was all Carmen gave her.

"I need help." Jas brought on the waterworks. "They froze my accounts. I don't have anybody. I need you to get me out of here."

Carmen gave her a quick reminder. "I tried to do that, remember? I came to the club and talked to you. Do you remember what I said?"

"I'm sorry. I need you. I need help. You gotta get me out of here."

Carmen knew that's what Jas wanted. Weeks' worth of voicemail messages told her so. She also knew she was going to help her. The only reason she allowed Jas to stay locked up for as long as she did was to get some payback. "I'll see what I can do," she told her. "You're not coming to my house, though. I have an apartment in Brookstone you can stay in if I'm able to get you out. It's temporary. You're gonna get a job and get on your feet. After that, you're on your own."

"Thank you, Carmen. Thank you so much."

The conversation continued for another minute before Tiara beeped in. Carmen didn't have any words to say to her, but she took the call anyway. The drama with Jay had her so consumed it made her issues with Tiara miniscule.

"I saw you resigned," Tiara began. "I knew you wanted to do it, but to see it…" Her voice trailed off. "I saw everything on the news. I'm sorry, Carm. I didn't know what I was doing. I didn't know Dumati was lying about being Carlos' brother. I would've never given him a ticket if I knew."

"I believe you," Carmen replied. "I'm over that. I put a bullet in his head. What I'm not over is what you did to my kids." Carmen sat up in bed. "We have our issues, but I would never mistreat Robin because we're arguing. You took her out my home. I understand you not wanting to see me, but you can still have somebody drop her off. Rakim and Nyla miss their friend."

"It was Malik's decision. I followed my husband's lead."

"I'll deal with him then," was Carmen's initial response. She followed it with, "It really doesn't matter that Robin's not here. The kids are in Puerto Rico with Jay. When they come back, we need to set up a play date. If Malik doesn't feel comfortable with Robin being in my home, I hope he's okay with my kids being in his. I want our kids to stick together. They're innocent in all this."

"I agree," Tiara replied. "Give me a call when they get back." A pause ensued. "The press release is going out soon, but I wanted to tell you personally. I'm launching my own company. It's called Goddess. I took your advice and I'm starting a line for little girls. I'm working with a slew of new talent, and I think I have something big."

"If it's coming from you, it is."

Despite their issues, Carmen wanted Tiara to be successful. She wanted Tiara out her shadow although she never thought her friend was there. She only prayed that when Tiara climbed the ladder of success, there wouldn't be a second-in-command, waiting to backstab her.

TWENTY

Two Days Later

Carmen didn't see the beige car outside her front gate until she pulled up beside it. She spent most of the morning communicating with the lawyer she found for Jas and was still on the phone with him. Their conversation ended right as a man stepped out the beige car. She rolled her window down when she saw the yellow manila envelope in his hands.

"Carmen Santiago?" he asked.

She held her hand out as she knew she was being served. Gomez's recent phone calls prepped her for it. "Give it to me," she told him when she sensed his hesitation. "I got somewhere to be." She was headed to a doctor's appointment to confirm a suspicion. He put the envelope in her hand only for Carmen to toss it in the passenger seat. She then took off down the road.

The envelope stayed in that spot until she retrieved it almost two hours later. She was sitting in the parking lot of Brookstone Women's Health. As much as she wanted to toss the envelope out the window and drive over it, she didn't. She read the papers, word for word, her anger growing by the minute. The first thing that set her off was learning Jay filed on the grounds of adultery. While her infidelity caused the end of their marriage, the filing put their business in the streets. Once TMZ got wind, she was back on the blog sites and on the front page of *Star*.

That was only half of the worst. The other half was his request for full legal and physical custody of Rakim and Nyla. That set her ablaze. That sent her calling his phone. Silvas answered, and she told him to give the phone to Jay. He declined, but she wasn't in the mood to hear no. "Give him the phone or I'm flying to Puerto Rico and I'm shooting my way inside." Those words got Jay on the phone. However, the sound of his voice changed her mindset. It reminded her of the bigger picture. "I called to tell you off," she began. "I had the words planned out of what I was gonna say. I'm not gonna give it to you. Or at least not all of it. I will say this. You filed like this to embarrass me."

"You fucked him, didn't you?" Jay raged.

"I know my sins," she whispered. She closed her eyes as tears formed. Her mind went back to the day of her anniversary party. It was a January morning. She left Jay in the glam room while she went to shower. "I know my sins," she repeated. "Why does the world have to know them, too?" Jay's figure appeared in her mind.

He stared at her, not in awe, but like he was preparing to attack. His narrowed eyes and gritted teeth reminded her of a lion on the prowl. He stripped himself of his clothes, a sign the lion found its prey.

"I'm not going to argue with you," she continued, opening her eyes. "I want to be at peace."

His stare was a fiery mix of aggression and pain. He knew what he was doing. He tightened his grip around her neck to hold her in place. At that moment, it came. The final thrust in which he unleashed his power inside her.

"Right now," she told him. "I don't have the energy to fight you. I need to focus on other things and this divorce isn't it. If you want Rakim and Nyla, you can keep them." She tasted the tears that fell on her lips. "Because I'm gonna keep the two you put inside of me."

Carmen didn't give him a chance to respond. She didn't care what he had to say. Whether good or bad. She tossed her phone in the passenger seat on top of the divorce papers. The tears were still coming. She cried for multiple reasons. The first was the blessing she received from God. After suffering two back to back miscarriages, each child she lost was back in her womb. While they would be born during a divorce, joy came from knowing they were there.

Now on her way home, Carmen knew what awaited her. She had to tell Kane she was pregnant. She knew what the news would do. The news would break him. And it did. The one thing he kept asking her is why was she giving Jay two.

"Two?" Kane was bawling his eyes out. "You're giving him two? He deserves two?"

They were standing in the foyer alone. He repeated the question over and over although she didn't have a response to give him. The conversation ended with him punching a mirror and leaving.

Two days later, Carmen was sleeping peacefully when a mix of voices, thuds, and bangs woke her up. The first thing she did was grab her cell. She checked the security cameras in the foyer and saw Gully and Linx on the screen. Gully was holding Rakim while Linx had Nyla. Both kids were asleep. They proceeded to climb the steps. In the meantime, Roman and Cesar lugged in suitcases and boxes. Their presence told her Jay wasn't far behind.

Minutes later, Silvas appeared. When she saw Jay's butler, she put her phone down. She could hear Gully and Linx as they placed Rakim and Nyla in their rooms. She then heard Jay's walker outside her bedroom window. The noise led her to her closet. She grabbed a small bag before getting back in bed.

Small enough to fit in her palm, the bag became hidden once she made a fist. With a firm grip on it, she closed her eyes.

Carmen didn't know how long she'd slept. All she knew was that when she opened her eyes, it was still pitch black outside. She also wasn't alone. Jay's frame was at the foot of the bed. In quick spurts, every threat he gave her echoed in her ears. The slurs came, too.

From the way he stared at her, something told her she wasn't going to hear those words. Unsure of what he was there to do, Carmen stared him down. Their eyes remained locked even as he stripped down to his boxers. He then took them off. The sight of his manhood sent a tingle between her legs. It also reminded her of the dream he said he had.

Is he here to make up? Or is he teasing the idea? Is this a mind game?

A new thought came to mind. To even get to Brookstone, Jay had to show Silvas he was stable. There was a strong possibility the news of their twins brought him out the manic episode. Everyone knew, the one thing he wanted more than anything was another baby. They were fresh into the New Year when he told her he wanted seven more kids. She got him to compromise on one. If it was God's Will, in the fall, she would birth two.

Jay believed the gift needed reciprocation. She saw it when his hand wrapped around his manhood. The stroke he gave it told her he wanted her. He also did it to test her. She could hear his inner thoughts. He knew what he'd said to her like she knew what she'd done to him. He questioned if she could look over it. Carmen couldn't, but she could ignore it long enough to celebrate their blessing. To show him she would oblige, she pulled the covers back. His shoulders relaxed as if he caught the hint. Then, he looked away. Carmen followed his gaze. The bag was still in her hand. Her tight fist gave him the impression she was on guard. She loosened her grip to settle his nerves. It wasn't enough. Therefore, she unclenched her hand, the velvet bag now visible.

Unbeknownst to Jay, she had stolen from Kane. She was certain her ex knew it, too. He chose for some reason not to speak on it. She wouldn't either. Or at least not to him. The indiscretion fell on Jay's ears. The conversation started with kisses to her lips, kisses to her chest, and soft kisses to her womb. Jay went deep inside her, his breath falling on her skin as he panted from the intensity. Once his seed was spilled, she massaged the back of his neck, calming him from the high. His head then rested on her stomach as if he could hear their babies' heartbeats.

Overcome with emotion, a tear streamed down his face, landing underneath her navel. It signaled her to loosen the bag's strings. She then brought the bag closer to his face. He stared at her hands as she turned the bag over, dumping the contents inches from where he laid. The red stones put a spark in his eyes, yet the Pink Sunrise took his breath.